Mercy

Somerset University

Ruby Vincent

Published by Ruby Vincent, 2020.

Prologue

"I'm not sure they want me there."

"This party wouldn't be happening if it wasn't for the hard work you put in." Maverick snaked his arm around my waist, resting his chin on my shoulder, and smiling at me in the mirror. "You're at the top of the guest list, Val."

"Don't think Ortega and Kessler feel the same way," I muttered. "Jade only deals with me for house business and Kessler doesn't return my calls."

"We're on to them now. We couldn't find a trace of half of those students who dropped out. They're avoiding you, so they can't be caught saying or doing anything incriminating."

I met his eyes in the mirror, a grim twist to my lips.

In the weeks since Bianca attacked, I retreated into the safety of my boys and friends, letting the police do their work. As a result, the rest of my semester was somewhere approaching normal—a word not often ascribed to my life. I say approaching normal because in the background was Maverick, searching for people who left no trace behind.

I smoothed the chiffon gown, rippling over the beaded bodice. The night of my charity dinner had arrived. The decorations I chose transformed the ballroom. The menu I approved was whipped up in the kitchen. Blair and I collected and organized the prizes. This was my party and Maverick was correct, I had every right to be there, but...

"It'll be hard to smile and trade small talk about the weather now that we know what we do. I just wish I knew what to do now."

"The only thing we can do is prove something awful happened to them," said Maverick. "The first step is getting into that file on Aiden's computer. We'll find Teagan and Sawyer, Val."

"If it's not too late," I whispered.

I finished getting ready and the two of us met Ezra, Jaxson, Ryder, Gwen, and her boyfriend, Max, downstairs.

Gwen was bouncing in her floor-length teal gown. "I can't believe we're going to a party at the Evergreen Country Club. Where are you taking me next week, Jaxson?"

He blew out a breath. "When do I trade my groveling for your forgiveness? Lunch has been on me every day for weeks."

"You accused me of being a violent, obsessed attempted killer because how could I not be in love with you?" She rolled her eyes, snuggling into Max. "You're going to be buying me paninis for a long time."

Jaxson mumbled something I couldn't hear but earned him a laugh and playful whack on the arm from Gwen.

Not only their friendship recovered from Bianca. Daniel Meyer was also on the mend. Banged up in the car crash, he took time off to rest with his family, but if the rumors were true, he planned to attend the charity dinner and snag that two-week tropical vacation.

We headed out to the cars, driving the short trip to the country club. The place was packed. The parking lot was fit to burst, and couples and coeds dressed in their finest streamed inside the club. We drove up to the valet. Maverick got out and opened my door, holding his arm out to me.

"Ready?"

"I'm ready."

I climbed out and we melded into our group, passing through the frosted double doors and stepping on the red velvet carpet winding through the lobby for the ballroom. The carpet was Aiden's idea. Seeing it in action, I kind of liked it.

"Any prize in particular you want, Val?" Maverick asked. "We could snag that tropical vacation for ourselves."

"If this was one of those win-a-man auctions, I'd put a couple million on you." I covertly pinched his backside.

Maverick laughed. "I go for a lot more than that. Good thing you get all of this for free."

"Lucky me." I rose on tiptoe, claiming a kiss.

"Valentina? Oh, Valentina. There you are."

We broke apart. Jade scurried out of the ballroom, resplendent in a slinky black gown, and held her hands out for me.

"Is something wrong?" I asked as she took them. There must be. Jade's barely spoken to me in weeks.

"Yes, there is and it's me. I was wrong for how I reacted to your idea to invite all the past brothers and sisters."

I pulled a face. What did she just say?

"I'm sorry. What?"

"Tonight is about the Zeta Rho and Nu Alpha family coming together to do good for our community," she said. "And our family doesn't stop at those who graduated with us."

Jade tucked my hand under her arm and drew me inside. The ballroom was even more magnificent than I pictured. A wonderland of gold and white, draped in elegance for the mingling alumni to enjoy. I spotted Sofia among one such group, but Jade tugged me on before I could think to go to her.

"Once I realized I was being silly," Jade continued, "I took up your task."

"My task?"

Jade stopped behind a group of people and tapped a shoulder covered in blue ruffles. "Say hello to our new president."

The woman turned. My breath caught, held by the fist that punched my gut. Eyes gaping, I looked at her, connecting the person before me with the one I met over a year ago and coming up with one name.

Teagan Kainer.

"Teagan?"

"Hi," she said cheerily. "It's great to see you again. I can't believe the hopeful I talked to all those months ago is now the president who organized this. Isn't it amazing, babe?"

The guy next to her faced me, sliding his arm around her shoulder. Sawyer Burn smiled even wider than Teagan. "Incredible. Hey, is Ezra around?" he asked. "We've gotta catch up."

I couldn't answer. Couldn't think. Couldn't comprehend what I was seeing in front of me.

"I'm so happy they accepted the invite," Jade said. There was a blatant note of triumph lacing her voice. What she had won, I had no idea.

She gripped my hand tighter.

"Once a sister, always a sister."

Chapter One

M*averick*

Val was whisked away from me so fast, I lost her in the crowd.

The party was for the alumni of Zeta Rho Sigma and Nu Alpha Theta. As I scanned the crowd, I noticed that included a fair amount of Evergreen's high society. I wanted to believe this many influential people couldn't be involved in the mystery behind this Greek façade. I wanted to, but I better than anyone knew that secrets were woven in the thread of this community. It's basically what it was founded on.

There.

A wisp of blue chiffon caught my eye. I veered away from an incoming server and made a beeline for Valentina, seeking her bobbing head over the crowd.

"Ricky."

A hand on my shoulder pulled me up short. I barely got the greeting out before my dad slammed me to his chest, pounding me on the back, and rumbling me with his laugh. He released me only for Mom to move in.

"Hi, sweetie." She kissed my cheeks and then pulled out her handkerchief to wipe off the lipstick. "This party is something. Valentina did an amazing job. Where is she? We want to congratulate her. You're sitting at our table, aren't you? I feel like I hardly ever see you. Why don't you come home this weekend?"

My mother's rapid-fire questions pelted me from all angles. It was her gift to mix a little guilt in there too. "Val ran that way. I'll catch her up and then we will be sitting with you. How about I come over on Saturday and spend the day? Adam will love running around with the dogs."

Mom smiled—satisfied. It was in her smile that I saw our resemblance. I looked so much like my father that Mom and Dad called me "mini-me" most of my life. For a while, I thought it was my given name. His clone I might be, but her baby boy I was always. It took a few tries to slip out of her embrace and return to tracking down Val.

The ballroom was filling up as more people arrived, and the last place I spotted her was taken up by a gaggle of her sorority sisters—one of them Sofia.

I stepped in that direction and the crowd parted. There she was.

Standing next to the short woman in the black dress who whisked her away, Val was deep in conversation with a couple whose faces were angled out of my sight. As I watched, Val grasped the lady of the couple's hand and drew her to the side. The shorter woman tried to follow, but Valentina put her hand up with the stern set to her jaw that I spotted from halfway across the room. The woman stopped and let Valentina lead her captive to the far corner of the room next to the stage. She might as well have shouted something was going on.

I took off, converging on her in time to hear the tail end of her sentence. "—happened to you, Teagan?"

Teagan? As in Elizabeth Teagan Kainer?

The woman from the defunct Facebook page smiled. There was no doubt it was her. I'd been searching for a digital trace of her for months and there she stood in front of Val, head cocked and nose scrunched like she didn't understand the question.

"What do you mean?" she asked.

"Val." I went to her side, sliding a protective arm around her waist. "What's going on?"

"That's what I'd like to know," she said. "Teagan, you disappeared."

She made a low noise in her throat. "I know. I totally vanished off the face of the earth. I didn't want to leave school but my mom passed away and then—" She turned away, eyes bright. "I just couldn't deal, you know. With anyone or anything."

"That's not what I mean," Val said.

Teagan frowned. "What?"

"I'm sorry about your mother. Of course I am. I understand if that's what took you away, but that's not the story I heard."

"What did you hear?" she asked slowly.

"That you were kidnapped."

The blunt statement flared Teagan's eyes.

"You were taken by a 'they' who then told the Sallys and Sams what to say to cover your disappearance."

Teagan scoffed, throwing me an incredulous look screaming *"what the hell is she talking about?"*

"Valentina, I don't—"

"My boyfriend overheard Aiden Connelly in his basement saying that you had to be taken. And the guy you were just snuggling with—the one who swore he didn't have a clue who you were after you disappeared—was the next to go just like Aiden said he would. In his case, my boyfriend saw him snatched and driven off in a van. I've been looking for both of you for months and I couldn't find anything. Not a tweet. Not a working home number. Nothing to prove if you were alive or dead. So, I ask again, Teagan, what happened to you?"

Teagan's jaw hung open. She stared at her with confusion and disbelief etched into the lines marring her smooth face and I was studying her every twitch and blink.

Seems like she truly doesn't know what Val's talking about... and that's proof enough that something is very wrong here.

"Nothing happened, Valentina. I wasn't— wasn't *taken*!" she cried. "I left because I was grieving for my mother."

"Why did Sawyer Burn swear he didn't know anyone named Teagan after you left?" I couldn't help asking.

Teagan turned on me. "Maybe because I ended things with him abruptly and he was upset. When I felt better, I called him and we got back together."

"What number did you call?" Val asked. "Because Ezra and I tried every number we could find and couldn't reach Sawyer."

"He got a new phone."

"Teagan." Val stepped forward, dropping her voice. "I'm not accusing you of anything. I know something happened to both of you. Something that I believe has happened to other people who left the Sallys and Sams and were never heard from again. You can tell me what's going on," she whispered. "I'll believe you. I'll help you."

Teagan shook her head. "If someone kidnapped me, the first thing I'd do with my freedom is go to the police. Not a charity dinner. Now, I came here to have fun and hang out with my friends who I haven't seen for a long time." She sidestepped us. "I'm done with this bizarre conversation."

We let her go without a word. What else could we do?

"Do you believe her?" I asked.

"No, Maverick. Something's wrong. Very wrong." The words settled like lodestones in my stomach. "I was digging. Asking too many questions. Then Jade unearthed those two and presented them to me with a self-satisfied smirk she couldn't contain. Just like that, we're the crazy people shouting about disappearances and that's exactly what people will believe if we don't let it go."

"Val, what are we supposed to believe?" My gaze trailed Teagan through the crowd. She secured Sawyer in a hug and dropped a kiss on his smiling lips. "Those two aren't missing. There isn't a scratch on them and Teagan is repeating the same story you were given. They don't look like victims of a sinister fraternity plot to me."

"If they're not the victims... maybe they're a part of it."

"A part of what, Val? What in the hell is going on here?"

"Whatever it is has to be connected to that hidden file on Aiden's computer. Are you closer to getting in?"

"It's encrypted like I've never seen before. They haven't invented the means to crack it, which is why I will. I'll figure out how to open that file, but, Val." I turned her to face me. "Whatever is in that file, it's not Grandma's secret banana bread recipe. He went through extreme lengths to protect that file and extreme measures might be taken if he finds out we're trying to get into it. I'm asking you again, drop out of this sorority."

"I can't do that," she replied—like I knew she would. "Maverick, Sawyer was thrown in the back of a van and sped off to who-knows-where. Now he's sipping cocktails and smiling like it never happened. Something is going on that we can't comprehend right now, but Sofia and our sisters are not getting caught up in it. I have to stay and watch out for them."

It wasn't a strong hope that she'd agree with me. All the same, I'd never forgive myself if I didn't ask and keep asking. I wanted to know the truth, but I wanted Val safe more.

She placed her hand over my heart. "Focus on cracking the file. I'll find out more from Teagan, Sawyer, and Jade. We will find the truth. I promise."

"I promise," I said, "to protect you. That's the promise I care about."

She kissed me—slow, sweet, and mind-scrambling.

I couldn't pull her away from the Sallys, but I would make sure none of those picture-perfect coeds laid a hand on her.

I'll find out what you're hiding, Aiden. Then the bomb will drop... on you.

Chapter Two

Six Months Later

Valentina

"The deejay should be here at nine. We've got sisters on the chips, dip, veggies, and beer. I'll start on the sliders and cookies as soon as I finish with the balloons."

"After this I'll move the breakables to my room," Blair said. "Whenever we open the party to the entire row, I swear those guys make a bet to see how much of our stuff they can trash."

Laughing, I poked my head in the kitchen, confirmed the girls were laying out the spread, and continued to the back door, Blair on my heels. "What can we do? It's their graduation party. The seniors wanted all their friends to come."

"I feel like it's been an endless cycle of events, parties, theme nights, and bonding activities since the charity dinner," she said. "That event was definitely our best, though. My mom's still talking about it. Asking me if we'll throw it every year."

I fell silent. Scanning the backyard and the sisters putting out the tiki torches and hanging lights saved me from answering.

Our Christmas charity dinner was a big hit. The brothers, sisters, and alumni were bouncing out of their finery to see old friends again. It wasn't just Sawyer and Teagan who made a triumphant return. Most of the people Maverick, Sofia, and I dubbed missing were somehow located by Jade Ortega and accepted her invite. As that night wore on, my confidence in what I thought I knew was shaken to the core.

And all this time later, I still don't know what to believe.

How could I when the proof that the Sallys and Sams didn't hurt those people was standing right in front of me, beaming and telling stories of their vibrant lives free of deep, dark holes?

"It only gets more intense from here," I finally said. "Next year, we have pledges. Innocent young hopefuls ready to become the next generation of Sallys. I wonder how many Blairs will be in that bunch."

She dropped her clipboard to playfully smack my arm. "If you mean brilliant, driven, hardworking women, then I say we'll get a lot of Blairs."

"Modest," I mused. "That's what I always liked about you."

We cracked up.

The truth was Blair and I sailed through our final semester of sophomore year, running the Sally house like a well-oiled machine. All those parties, events, theme nights, and bonding activities we organized and led together. Somewhere along the way we became friends for real. The two of us kept the house afloat.

"Ladies, what do you think?" Jade waved across the lawn where she was hanging up the final string of lights.

The two of us—and Jade.

My house mother did a one-eighty since the night of the fundraiser. The pinched lips and narrowed eyes fled in return of her million-watt smile and constant offers to take the stress off my plate. I knew there was more behind that smile. But there was nothing else for me to do except wait, watch, and run my house.

"Looks great," I called.

I went back inside, continuing my sweep.

"Just a little higher on your side, Carmen."

Carmen rose on tiptoe, balancing on the kitchen stool. She inched the banner up and taped it over the living room entrance. "Congratulations, Seniors!" spelled out in shiny gold letters.

One of the most baffling, insane school years had come to an end and the house demanded to celebrate it in style. The seniors were moving on and almost one-third of the Sallys and Sams were set to walk across the stage.

Aiden Connelly would not be one of them. He was in his fourth year of university. It just so happened that a prodigy like him easily juggled football, the presidency, friends, and an accelerated five-year program to earn his bachelor's and master's in mathematical finance. I had one more year with Aiden, and it was my last chance to discover the truth about him and the night he sent Sawyer to the van.

"Val, do any of the Sams have a peanut allergy?" Palmer poked her head out of the kitchen. "Teagan and I were thinking Thai."

Teagan.

I had to learn the truth from Aiden because it definitely wasn't coming from Teagan. She managed to earn readmission to our university due to unforeseen circumstances forcing her to leave. Sally house couldn't turn her down after the admissions office welcomed her with open arms, so for the last six months, the very girl who recruited me lived upstairs in her old room. And the entire time she stuck to her story.

I cocked a brow. "You're supposed to be thinking sour cream chips and soda."

"I forget to turn the oven off one time—"

"Three times."

"—and you ban me from cooking. Well, I'm going to show you my skills, Moon. Get ready for this."

"You have to get me ready for something else," I replied. "Three Sams have peanut allergies."

She nodded. "It's cool. I can make shrimp lettuce wraps sans nuts."

"You can wrap deez nuts!" one of the girls shouted from the kitchen.

They busted up in there, howling so loud I felt my phone before I heard it. I fished it out and checked the screen.

"Hey, Maverick."

Maverick.

His parents, family, and the boys called him Rick or Ricky. I'd always call him Maverick. I couldn't help it. The way my tongue caressed the name and rolled it from my lips was almost too intimate for company.

"What's up?" I asked. "Is robotics practice over?"

"I'm not at robotics. I'm in the library." The hushed tone made sense. "Val, you have to get over here— Or I'll come to you."

My brows drew together. "Is everything okay?"

"I'm in, Val. In Aiden's file. I hacked it."

MAVERICK

I paced the study room. Back and forth in the closet of a space—interrupted by my shooting to the desk to check again.

Val arrived exactly twenty minutes after I called her. She blew in on a cloud of rose perfume and kissed me, soothing my agitation the way only she could.

"You did it?" she asked, turning to the laptop. "It's been months. How did you get in?"

"I'm sorry it took so long." I pulled out a chair for her to sit. "I know how serious this is, but I had to go slow. Use outside networks. Mask my IP address. Consult three different hackers. One of whom didn't speak English."

Val rubbed the back of my neck. She knew the struggles I had butting against the first program I didn't know how to hack. It was long nights at my desk while she rubbed my shoulders, testing how long I'd hold out until my need for her pulled me to bed. After she fell asleep, I went back to my desk to wrestle with the file again.

"I've never seen code like this," I said. "The protections he had on this file were smart. Adaptive. One wrong move and it'd alert Aiden to an intrusion, plus learn my technique to shut me out permanently. I had to invent the code to crack this thing, Val." Blowing out a breath, I drew the laptop to us. "Patenting it will bring us from ridiculously wealthy to obscenely wealthy. Adam's getting diamond-studded sneakers for his birthday."

She laughed. "I don't know about Adam, but Mommy wouldn't mind some diamonds."

Despite myself, I grinned. No matter the circumstance, Val lit up my worst days. "I'll get you a whole truckload. It'll make up for what I found."

Her cheeriness leeched away. "It's blackmail, isn't it?" she croaked. "All of the *secrets* he collected, used to silence people like he did with Ezra and get rid of them like Sawyer. It's the only reason I can think of for why Sawyer refuses to admit he was hauled off in that van against his will."

"No— I mean, yes." I tapped the pad, bringing up the file. "The secrets he collected on the Sams are in here," I confirmed. "But what he's doing with the information isn't. And that's the only thing that's not in here."

"What does that mean?"

I navigated to a tab labeled "freshmen" and a list of names rolled down the screen. I clicked one at random and leaned back for Val to read.

She squinted at the information—face wrinkled with curiosity, then confusion, then shock, and finally the emotion I settled on: horror.

"What the fuck is this?!"

"Notes," I said. "Pages and pages of detailed notes on every freshman in the Sam house. Eating habits, sleeping habits, weight loss, weight gain, grades, study habits, classes, friends, family, background, career plans, and how they respond to different situations."

Val's cheeks drained of color as I rattled off the list.

"It's not just the freshmen," I continued. "He's got a file on everyone in the Sam house and look at this." I clicked a folder labeled *training camp*. "That trip you and Ezra went on—where you ran the obstacle course. Read some of the things he wrote."

"Davidson paused and looked back when his opponent fell," she read. "Nicolas climbed with perfect technique. Nathan didn't throw the race to let his girlfriend win. Jose showed anger after his loss." Val turned to me. "I don't understand this. It was a friendly game over who'd pay for spring break vacations. All he needed to write down was who won or lost. Why would he record all of this? Why pay attention to who looked back or got angry?"

"You mentioned that Leighton and Aiden seemed intent, huddled together over their clipboards and talking in hushed tones. That obstacle race was clearly about more than who won the bet. He calls it a training camp."

"Training for what?" she asked, mostly to herself.

Valentina clicked back to the freshmen folder. She fell silent as she scanned the info and then looked through the other grades as well. "Pledge points," she spoke up.

"What?"

"Most of this is the criteria Aiden said he uses to assign pledge points, but this is on a stalker-level scale. The stuff that he's dug up on these guys. Not just one secret. He has all the secrets. Dirt that would put them and their families six feet under."

"He's hacking them," I said. "Maybe even tapping phones."

"It doesn't say what he does with the information except for one or two cases." She pointed. "Look. Aiden discovers one of the guys' fathers is in possession of child porn and he anonymously reported it to the police."

"What's the guy's name?"

"Donald Seward."

I quickly looked him up. "Yeah, I've got a record of his arrest."

"There's another guy he found out was taking up-skirt shots of unsuspecting girls. Says he was dropped from the Sams and another anonymous message was sent to the dean. Seems like Aiden is capable of doing the right thing."

"Don't raise your opinion of him yet, Val." I pulled up a chair, sitting next to her. "He discovered Brian was being threatened by the Sons of Slaughter and he wasn't moved to report that. He blackmailed Ezra to keep his mouth shut."

She nodded, lips pursed. "If he's making a habit of blackmail, there's nothing in here about it. No records of payments or favors. All there is are checkmarks next to the secrets that will be used to test loyalty."

"But it can't just be about that," I argued. "Tracking what they eat and searching out gang connections is bigger than getting into a silly fraternity. What does all of this look like to you?"

"Sleeping habits. Grades rising or falling while in the Sams. Tracking their health and stamina through the physical requirements. Honestly... if I didn't know better, I'd say these were files you'd keep on lab rats."

I bobbed my head, observing the dozens of tabs holding even more names. "I had the same disturbing thought."

"Do you think this information is going to someone? The *they* Aiden spoke about in the basement. I can't believe he woke up one day and decided to do all of this for shits and giggles."

"That's even more disturbing."

"Who would want to know these things?" she asked. "What do they do with it?"

I lifted my shoulders. "It's possible that Aiden doesn't record payments or favors because someone else is collecting."

"That would explain the digging for secrets. Not all of this other stuff. It's like the guys are in an unknown contest for who is the number one Sam."

I met her eyes. "I'm betting it's not just the guys."

"You think Leighton was keeping a file like this?"

"She dug into your lives like Aiden Connelly does. She had mysterious *friends* like Aiden as well."

"Maybe the same friends," she mused. "This doesn't explain why they covered up a murder for her. What were they getting out of their relationship with her that disposing of a body is a fair exchange? And she didn't doubt that they would. That night, she was calm and cool. The three of them came with me ready and willing to kill Logan, and Leighton said her *friends* would clean it up like it was a given. Almost like they'd done it before."

My fists balled. "It's frustrating that we still don't know enough to answer that. Six months and all I've confirmed is what we already know: Aiden has an ulterior motive behind everything he's doing. What that motive is, we still have no clue."

Val rubbed my forearm. "We haven't gone through everything. There may be something here. Did you read the notes he kept on Sawyer Burn?"

"The first thing I looked at after I realized what this was. Aiden has the same details on him that he does on the other guys. They go up to the night he disappeared, but there's nothing on where he was taken, why, or by whom. It's not even mentioned. The final entry is a note on his improved running times."

She blew out a breath. "It'd be too much to ask that he offer up the incriminating evidence. All right, send me all of this, please." Val got to her feet. "The only way to go from here is to confront him with his stalker profiles. I can't wait to see him try to talk his way out of this."

"What? Val, no." I darted up and intercepted her at the door. "You can't tell him we got into his file."

"Why not?"

"Because of what you just said. Those files are disturbing but we don't have anything we can take to the police. There's no proof he's blackmailing anyone. We can't even argue that he's protecting dangerous people because he reports the worst things he finds. All Aiden has to say is he's overzealous about ensuring the Sams remain up to standards and the cops will wave him out of the door."

"Then he can try giving that explanation to me. I'll watch his face as he spins bull about the president needing to know how many calories our brothers and sisters eat. He can fool everyone else but he can't fool me."

Val made to sidestep me. I moved in sync with her.

"More reason why you can't say anything." I gripped her shoulders, drawing her into my worried gaze. "Aiden went to extreme lengths to hide those records. He might be able to offer an innocent explanation to everyone else, but he knows you're onto him. Ezra connected him to Sawyer's disappearance. He overheard him say other people were involved, and now we've found this file. Whoever *they* are, they have no problem with making people disappear, and if they find out you know too much, they'll decide you're next." I pulled her to my chest. "I'm not letting that happen."

She rested her head on my chest. "Okay, then what do we do?"

I couldn't temper my relief at her agreement. I prepared myself to put in hours of convincing. I said as much. "I thought you'd fight me harder on this."

"I can fully admit that we have no idea what we're dealing with. We don't know who, why, or how far this goes. Jade Ortega was off living her life free of the Sallys, but when Leighton *died*, she was quick on the scene to keep the house in line. I've never seen anyone more satisfied with themselves than she was the night of the charity dinner. She threw my accusations in my face and slammed home that I wasn't seeing the bigger picture.

"The fact is we're dealing with someone or someones who are clever, resourceful, and a few steps ahead. How do we catch up?"

"Tonight we'll comb through the entire file. There could be something we missed. From now on—and I know I've said this before—keep your distance from Aiden Connelly."

"Maverick—"

"Hear me out," I asked.

It took her a sec, but she nodded.

"You've watched him for two years and he hasn't given up a clue to who he's working with," I said. "We haven't even found them in his hidden file and I'm not counting on a second look turning up their names. He's too careful. Aiden isn't going to offer up a way in. But you know who might, Teagan and Sawyer. They were both taken—for all that they deny it. They're the ones we need to pay attention to. Find out where they've truly been." I rubbed her back. "Stick close to Teagan. If she's being threatened to keep quiet, she may eventually open up to a friend. To you."

Val hummed. "That's code for sit back, hang out, and do nothing."

"See how well you know me."

A breathy laugh escaped her. "I do have to remember Sawyer and Teagan are the victims in all of this. That file alone proves Aiden, or *they*, collect plenty of ammo to keep people in line. Aiden forced Ezra to keep quiet about the Sams. Teagan could be under the same pressure."

"We will figure out what the hell is going on and put a stop to it. I promise."

She squeezed me tight. "I know we will."

VALENTINA

"All this stuff is making my head spin. I don't know what to think anymore." Sofia stopped in front of a stable. A long muzzle and tawny head poked over the door, sniffing out the treats in her pocket. Sofia murmured to the horse as she passed over the last of her apple slices.

I moved to the other side, gently running my fingers through her mane. The weekend brought a trip to the Richards Estate and a visit with Adam's horse. He and Madeline were in the stall a few doors down. He wasn't old enough to ride her yet, but Madeline was happy to start teaching him how to care for her.

I wished I could enjoy a lazy day with my son and best friend, but the conversation inevitably returned to the Sallys.

"Teagan came back like nothing happened," Sofia went on. "If she went through a traumatic experience, she's hiding it better than I've ever seen. Could we have been wrong? Is it possible she was home coping with her mother's death and cut everyone off to deal?"

"I want to believe that, and I would if not for what Ezra overheard in the basement. One of the guys was freaking out over pretending Teagan didn't exist. Why would you have to pretend a girl grieving for her late mother didn't exist?"

"That's true," she said under her breath. "Plus, there's no good explanation for tossing a guy in the back of a van and speeding off into the night. Did you and Maverick find anything that could help on Aiden's laptop?"

Sofia knew about our digging. I was keeping her up to date on everything.

"We went through the file twice, found out more than I ever wanted to know about the Sams of Nu Alpha, and none of it proved a thing other than Aiden's a dirt-digging creep. That much we knew already."

Sofia dusted off her hands, dropped a kiss on Peaches's nose, and linked arms with me, strolling through the stable. "Was the dirt in Sawyer's file bad enough that he'd keep his mouth shut about what really happened?"

I stiffened.

Aiden was meticulous in all things. Sawyer's file included the names of the adult films his father made in college, along with the locations of the VHS copies. The details of his teacher mother accepting bribes to change her students' grades were exact down to the parents who were able to meet her price. And that Sawyer broke down and cheated himself, buying a term paper in his freshman year.

If they did threaten him, swearing that he'd be kicked out of college, his mother would never work in another school, and the world would find out his father went bottoms up in a backyard gang bang, then that was decent incentive.

"That bad, huh?" Sofia asked softly.

"Bad enough." It wasn't the most shocking of the secrets I'd read, but that didn't mean he wanted it to get out. "I just wish I knew the truth. Why is Aiden keeping those notes? Is he doing it on someone else's orders? How do we find out the truth if Teagan won't talk to us?" I shook my head. "It's awful walking into the Sally house and wondering who will be next to disappear."

"That's not going to happen. Not with you and me around."

I threw her a skeptical look.

"I'm not just saying that to make you feel better," she said. We stepped out into the sun, soaking in the warmth as our shoes skimmed the grass, collecting dew on our soles. "They've gotten away with it for so long because no one noticed there was something off. Now we know.

"Ezra knows. Maverick, Jaxson, Ryder, and the army Ryder's family employs know that something is off. If one of our sisters goes missing, we won't rest until we know for sure they are where we're told they are. Doesn't make for a smooth kidnapping. While we're around, the Sallys will be safe."

"You're right," I said, injecting steel into my voice. "If a sister is so much as one day late coming back from summer break, I'm hunting her down. *They* are not getting another president to look the other way."

"Or a president's best friend."

I leaned on her shoulder, thankful for the millionth time that Sofia had my back.

"We're going into our junior year of college. Everyone else is gearing up for a summer conked out by the pool, and you and I are unraveling kidnapping plots. Sounds nuts when I say it out loud."

She laughed. "That's because it is, my friend. Our lives have been a roller coaster of weird since we met on the steps of Evergreen Academy. I blame you."

"What?" I cried, bursting out laughing. "It's not my fault. I'm dragged into it, I tell you. Dragged."

"Uh-huh." A smirk played at her lips. "Well, how about this? It's officially the first day of summer vacation. The Sally house is basically deserted and your presidential duties are on hold. The Sallys and Sams are safe in their homes. Teagan and Sawyer are alive. We have a break from worrying and stressing out about the secrets of Greek Row. For the next three months, let's cram so much normal summer fun into our lives that we're begging for weird by September."

"Deal."

We shook and linked pinkies over it.

My smile dimmed over our hands. "Can I bring up one more thing before we close the door on the topic?"

"What?"

"If Aiden is keeping the notes on the Sams, was Leighton doing it for the Sallys?" An edge leeched into my tone. "And after she left... did someone else take over?"

"You believe one of the Sallys is watching everything we eat, say, and do?" She shuddered. "If someone was clocking us like that, wouldn't we notice?"

I shook my head. "The way our bonding, house, and physical activities are set up, we're always in each other's faces. How would we know if someone was paying a little more attention than needed during the basketball game?"

Sofia considered it, eyes losing focus as the full implication that we were being watched set in, and she cringed like she felt their eyes on her then.

"I don't want to think about that right now," she cried. "The moratorium begins this second. You and I are relaxing today and for the next three months. Shopping, barbecues, movie nights, the whole thing."

I nodded along, taking my worries and locking them in the corner of my mind to be obsessed over as I lay in bed teetering on the brink of wakefulness and sleep.

"All I want to do right now is ride horses with my godson. He's gonna look so cute on top of Cinnamon in his full gear. Just wait till you see. I got him a helmet with his name on it."

My bobblehead jerked to a halt as that penetrated. "On top of Cinnamon?"

Sofia scurried off.

"Wait! Sof, he's too young to ride a horse!"

"Try and stop us, mama bear!"

I squawked, tearing after my insane best friend.

"LOOK HOW CUTE HE IS."

Caroline and I gushed over photos of Adam and Cinnamon on the terrace that night over a glass of wine (for her) and apple cider (for me).

Caroline's laugh tinkled into the evening. "Just look at that smile. That boy is going to break hearts with that smile alone, Val. Make no mistake."

I sighed. "I've accepted it. My baby reduced old ladies to puddles just by giggling in his stroller. I can't believe he's turning six."

"*I* can't believe you let him ride Cinnamon," she teased.

"I let him sit on Cinnamon while she remained completely still," I corrected. "After Sofia's wheedling, and Adam throwing me his big eyes, I broke down."

"It was worth it. Adam looks so happy. I tried to get Ryder interested in riding but he said he'd be asking for a lifetime taunted with bad puns with a name like his. Even as a little boy, my son was a wily one."

I chuckled. "Sounds like our Ryder. I never asked. How did you choose his name?"

"Ryder was... the name of someone very special to me."

The thought crossed my mind to ask if that someone was Ryder's true father. I kept it on the tip of my tongue. Caroline shared a lifetime worth of secrets with me. She offered me more trust than anyone ever had, and that included my boys. Anything else she decided to share would be on her terms. I'd never pry.

"Why did you choose Adam in the end?" she asked. "I remember you poring over baby books."

"Adam was a simple, uncomplicated name. Like I prayed his life would be."

Caroline reclined on the chaise, sweeping her feet up and taking the blanket I held out for her. She smiled up at the stars, basking in the beauty they reflected in each other. Caroline wore remission extremely well. Not that she didn't look like a supermodel even in the midst of her illness. But the color in her cheeks and the weight settling nicely on her bones did wonders for her.

She'd taken to spending every night on the terrace with me, a book, or a glass of wine. "Life is too short to be cooped up inside."

I copied her, letting out a relaxed sigh as I reached for my cider. "I had an ulterior motive for crashing your terrace time."

"Oh?"

"My mom flies in tomorrow," I began. "She's going home first to make sure the renters didn't trash the place and spend a few days getting situated. I was hoping after that she could come stay with us?"

"Valentina," she said. "You and Olivia know you don't have to ask. She can stay as long as she likes. She can move in if she wants to. We have plenty of extra rooms."

I laughed because I knew she was serious. "Apparently I'm the bird that stays very firmly in the nest. Just me, you, Adam, my mom, and my four boyfriends. One big happy family."

"We are one big happy family." She clinked our glasses. "I'd say you could move out and get a place of your own, but Ryder isn't interested in going too far from me and he's even less interested in you getting too far from him."

"I wouldn't make it past the driveway."

We giggled, nearly choking on our drinks.

A dry voice broke into our laughter. "I can sense you two talking about me."

"Is that what you think we do, my love?" Caroline replied. "Just sit out here gossiping about you." She shot me a wink.

"That's exactly what I think you do." Ryder lifted me without preamble and sat me in his lap, stretching us out on the chaise.

I buried my head in the crook of his neck, breathing him in. Ryder always smelled like spearmint spritzed with expensive cologne. It gave me the heady urge to throw him down and have my way with him. Mess up that perfectly coiffed hair. Rake my nails over his unblemished skin. And refuse to let up until he smelled of sex, sweat, and me, me, me.

"Are you warm enough, Mom?" he asked. "Want me to get you another blanket?"

"It's eighty degrees, dear." She stroked his cheek. "I'm fine. All I want is for you to tell me about your day."

"I met with the lawyers to discuss the buyout of Milkemoss Industries. It should move ahead without a problem. They also finished work on the day care. I was thinking I'd bring Adam in on Monday. He's got to walk around the office. Sit in the big chair that will one day be his."

Groaning, I said, "Don't. I was just moaning about my baby turning six. I can't picture him grown and taking over a company."

Ryder shrugged off his jacket and draped it over me. It was still eighty degrees but his instinct to take care of those he loved was strong.

"Is the party out here?" Jaxson poked his head out the sliding glass door. "Because I've got the food."

"Oooh. Then you're definitely invited," I said.

Jaxson swept out carrying a tray and was followed by Ezra and Maverick who were carrying one of their own.

"Mini empanadas, goat cheese bruschetta, and mille-feuille," he announced.

"Spanning the continents," I said. "I love it."

"What are we talking about?" asked Ezra.

Ryder fed me a piece of bruschetta. I answered around my mouthful. "Summer plans. My mom is coming to stay with us. Adam is stepping into his destiny, and Caroline and I are meant for more nights reclining on the terrace."

She held up her glass. "That we are."

Jaxson hopped on top of us, pulling a shriek out of me, and a growl from Ryder. He ignored my grumpy love and made himself comfortable. "We signed a new band, baby, and we've got a tour lined up for them next month. I'm not joining them for the entire thing but they've got a stop in New York I'm not going to miss. Want to come?"

"Is that even a question?" I popped a kiss on his lips. "Of course I want to come."

"Mom's letting me pitch this summer," Ezra added. "I might even get my own assignments."

"Has she forgiven you for getting yourself shot?" Jaxson asked.

"Most days."

"I'll be on campus." Maverick reached for the only part of me not covered by Jaxson or Ryder and ran a finger up my ankle. Goose bumps rippled along my skin. "The robotics team has a competition in the fall and we're behind on building the robot."

"Oh no," I said. "If we're not careful, we may have a normal summer that isn't plagued by crazed stalkers or lurking secret societies."

"Give it time, mama. Summer just started."

I flicked Jaxson's nose. "It's going to be great. We'll celebrate Adam's birthday, go to concerts, build robots, and do away with the craziness that's become our lives. We've earned it."

"I hear that," said Jaxson.

"Yep," Ezra threw in.

"Sign me up," Maverick said.

"And no more bodyguards," I added.

"Nope."

"No."

"No."

"Wrong, baby."

I heaved a sigh that lifted Jaxson's head. "I thought I'd sneak that in while we're all in a good mood. Guess we'll be arguing about that later."

"I'm looking forward to you losing that argument," Ryder said. The jerk took my cider and downed it. "You make the cutest face before you lob something at my head."

"Caroline should have made you ride a horse."

"What?" Ryder returned as his mother burst out laughing.

"I love this," she said. "Let's do it every night."

Chapter Three

Maverick
Val pulled up near the south entrance and killed the engine. She didn't need to chauffeur me around. I had three cars in perfect driving condition. But she offered to drive with one hand and give me a hand job with the other, and thus my ass was in the passenger seat in three seconds flat.

I had a weakness. Her name was Valentina.

"Bye, love." She leaned over and nuzzled my nose. "Build me a robot that will protect me when the evil ones take over."

I laughed. "Don't need a robot. That's my job."

Monday brought me back to campus. Val's next stop was home to pick up Adam and take him to Shea Industries. I had robots to build and a possible pickup game with a few guys from my flag football team. The ones that managed to drag themselves out of bed.

Cupping her cheek, I captured her lips in a kiss that quickly turned hungry. Her tongue wrapped around mine, drawing me in as her soft moans spread through my body. My cock twitched, waking up for another go.

Val was serious about us putting everything aside and enjoying our summer. So serious that whenever she caught me on my laptop, poring over Aiden's files, she stripped and gave me something else to focus on.

"What time should I pick you up?" she asked.

"I can bum a ride from one of the guys."

"Mom and I were thinking the three of us could go out to eat. She wants to catch up with you guys."

"In that case, we pack it up at one. Too late?"

"Nope. One is perfect." She kissed me again. "Now go so I can watch that tight ass walk away."

I shook my head, eyes falling shut. "You gotta stop objectifying me. I'm a man, not a piece of meat." I barely kept a straight face saying that and Val didn't try. She laughed me out of the car, landing a smack on my bottom as I stood. I strode off to her wolf whistles.

Grinning, I watched her over my shoulder. Seeing the naughty curve of her full lips clearer than anything on that sunlit day. Trailing the car as it pulled away and disappeared around a bend. The second she was gone, I wanted her back in my orbit.

People questioned everything about our relationship. I questioned one thing:

How she snuck up on me?

One day the new girl pulled up a stool next to me and the first strike was thrown.

I'd built walls for my walls. Cultivating the rep as the silent, brooding one. Hiding inside a helmet. Forcing myself to speak when spoken to and sometimes not even then. The more distance between me and the world, the less likely it would see the scars *she* left while I was too small and too weak to fight. That a few more years gave me the height, strength, and power I begged for was nothing short of a betrayal.

Too fucking late.

Now everybody could see me, but only Val came close. Bold and fearless and determined to figure me out like no one ever was. She drew laughs out of me after my mind forgot the sound. She intrigued me after I set in stone that people weren't worth my time. She pulverized wall after wall while I wasn't looking, and then one day I glanced up, and she was everywhere.

She was everything.

The robotics meeting was held in the computer engineering building in a lab on the third floor. I walked in, mind on Val, and vaguely noticed the guy coming down the opposite direction, heading for the same elevator.

I pressed the button as he stopped next to me.

"Hey. You're Ezra's friend, right?"

I looked down, though not far. Sawyer Burn wasn't as tall as me, but he was far from average height. "Burn?"

"Figured that was you." He held out his hand. "Didn't know if you remember me from the charity dinner."

"Yeah, I'm Maverick," I said slowly, extending my own for a shake. "I remember you. Ezra telling us how you were snatched off the street and driven off in a black van is hard to forget."

He winced. "I know how bad that looked, and I hate that Ezra lost his place with the Sams because he pushed to find me. I like that guy. Thought he'd make a great brother."

"Ezra isn't hung up about not getting into the fraternity. It's you he was worried about. He thought you were dead for a while."

"If I was snatched, I'm lucky Ezra would've had my back. As it is, I wish I could make it up to him."

You could do that by telling everyone the fucking truth.

I didn't bother saying it out loud. Sawyer was sticking to the story that his parents appeared out of nowhere and hauled him off. I didn't hold out hope that he'd break under the torture of lobby music and spill his guts as we waited for the elevator.

"You'll figure something out," I replied.

The elevator dinged.

I stepped in, pressed the button for the third floor, and propped myself against the handrail. Silence filled the small space.

My eyes fixed straight ahead, and out of the corner, I noticed him glancing at me. Quiet made others uncomfortable, but for me, it was home. I knew my way around an awkward silence like an Olympic runner knew his way around a track. I would not be the first one to—

"So where are you headed?" asked Sawyer as the doors opened. "Shouldn't you be off enjoying your summer vacation?"

"I have robotics."

"Seriously? Me too."

That didn't get an exclamation from me. I assumed we were going to the same place. Why else would he be here?

"I used to be on the team," Sawyer continued. "Had to drop out obviously. Mr. Frost let me back in and I'm taking summer classes to get back on track. It's like I never left."

I didn't take the bait, pretending like he left under normal circumstances and deserved a normal greeting welcoming him back.

I strode ahead of Sawyer, reaching our lab and holding the door open for him. "Glad to have you back, man."

And thank you for making it easy for me.

I returned his grin as he strode inside.

I wasn't meant to have a normal summer anyway.

VALENTINA

Adam bounced on Olivia's bed, chattering nonstop about everything that happened in his life since he last saw her. It had been less than a week since their Skype date. That was a lot in Adam time.

"Then Mommy took me to see Cinnamon and Miss Maddy let me brush her all by myself. I got to sit on Cinnamon and she was so big, Livia!"

"Cool," she gushed. "I can't wait to meet her. You can teach me how to ride."

"Okay!"

I leaned against the doorjamb, enjoying the scene. I promised my mom I'd graduate from Evergreen and then shower her in a life of luxury, and I kept my promises. My mom packed a suitcase shortly after I moved into Shea Mansion and set off around the world, visiting all the places she dreamed about from the other side of the television screen.

Adam and I missed her like crazy, but she was always a call away no matter the time zone.

And now she's home.

"You just gonna stand in the doorway? Get over here and give me some love."

Running to her, I threw myself in her hug. "I'm so glad you came up early. I thought you were staying in Wakefield for another week."

"I haven't seen my family in forever. Another week was torture," she said. "Where's my little man? Get in on this hug."

A squeal and then two tiny arms wrapped around our legs.

"Adam's hanging out with Daddy at his office today," I said. "After we drop him off, you and I are having lunch with Maverick." I released her to pick up Adam. He was getting too old to be carried and I didn't care. I'd hold him until he or my back complained. "Ready to go?"

"Yes. Livia, are you coming?"

"Of course, I am." Olivia tickled him, sending him into a squirmy, giggling fit. "I used to work at Shea Industries. I'll show you where they hide the good snacks."

"Yay!"

I carried Adam to his room, grabbed his stuff, and the three of us continued on to the car. The trip to Shea Industries wasn't a long one. Our twenty-five-minute drive we filled with music and chatter about Mom's trip.

"There are so many places the three of us have to visit together. Adam will love Hawaii. And you, Val, are destined for Egypt."

"It's Austria that's tempting me after seeing your pictures," I replied. "Speaking of, who were those gentlemen you were posing with, young lady?"

Mom tossed her head back laughing. "What happens on a transcontinental flight, stays on a transcontinental flight."

"Mom!"

Her cackling bounced through the car.

"Anyone I should know about?" I asked.

"Guillermo and I agreed to keep in touch, but it's not serious. Right now I'm focused on writing the next chapter in my life. I've been thinking a lot the last couple of months about going back to school."

"That's great, Mom. Will you finish your marketing degree?"

"I'm not sure. I enjoyed it, and when I worked for Shea Industries, I caught myself making mental notes on how I'd improve a presentation. I can still see myself doing it, but I don't have to fall into what's familiar. I'll poke around the community college catalog, audit a few classes, and see how I feel."

"Can I tell you that I always pictured you as a teacher or professor?"

"Honestly?"

I nodded as I switched lanes for the one heading directly to the company. "You're good with people. You know how to talk to them at their level. You don't take any nonsense, but you don't take yourself too seriously either. Plus, you said you look for and find ways that people can improve. What if you taught marketing, Mom?"

"Huh. That's not a bad idea." Mom tapped my forehead. "This is why I need you, kid. You put the pieces together for me."

"Did you talk to Caroline?" I asked. "She said you were welcome to stay indefinitely."

"Caroline is generous to a fault. I'd love to live with you and our favorite guy." Olivia twisted to smile at Adam. Adam beamed in return, showing off his missing-tooth smile. "But I have a home and friends in Wakefield. Evergreen Estates, promenades, and country clubs were never really my scene. I don't think I'd fit."

"Evergreenians are more down to earth than you think. Let Madeline get her hands on you. She'll introduce you to everyone and get you in on the parties and events. I want you to be a part of our life here, Mom."

She ran a finger along my cheek. "I'll always be a part of your life," she said. "But I like your idea. I'll get Caroline out of the house for a few wild girls' nights out. We'll shake things up. Blow the bow tie off this buttoned-up town."

"That is *not* what I suggested."

She busted up, inducing my eye roll. Had to love Olivia and her penchant for causing trouble.

We arrived at the company and Olivia and I brought Adam upstairs to Ryder's office. He rose from his desk as we came in and nearly fell back as Adam tackled his legs. Ryder snagged him around the waist and tossed him over his shoulder like a rolled-up rug.

"Ready to boss around a few underlings? Get your first firing out of the way?"

"Yes," Adam cheered.

I shook my head. "Why don't we start small and color Daddy pictures for his office while he works?"

"Okay." Adam sounded just as happy for the alternative.

Ryder put Adam on his feet. He ran off with Olivia to find the good treats while Ryder locked us in and got handsy with me on the couch. I untangled myself from him with difficulty when it was time to go.

Adam parked himself at the coffee table. Sunlight bathed him through the wall of windows, beating away shadows from the plush rug, leather sofa, bookshelves, and Ryder's desk which held not one or two, but three computer monitors.

Hard to believe all of this will be Adam's one day. I dropped a kiss on Adam's crown and ruffled his curls. He promised to draw me a picture too, and Mom and I headed out.

The drive to campus was a short one from Shea Industries. Maverick was stretched out on a bench waiting for us. From my seat I saw the glistening sheen of sweat boasting his game of football. Brains, brawn, looks, and a thick, ropey body that barely fit on the bench. Maverick Beaumont was the full package. And that package was mine.

He kissed me through the window. "Mind if we swing by the house so I can shower?"

"Sure. Mom and I are still arguing over what we want to eat."

"Thai," she spoke up. "I'm craving coconut curry soup."

"I had Thai a few days ago. If you want curry, let's get Indian."

"Maverick, you're the tiebreaker," said Mom.

He put his hands up. "Oh no. My place is never between my girl and my mother-in-law."

"Coward."

He laughed, leaning in to kiss me again. His lips brushed my cheek traveling to my ear. "Sawyer Burn joined the robotics team. He also followed me to the quad and announced he's joining the intramural team too."

My brows snapped together. "He did? Well, he does have a lot of catching up to do after missing a year and a half."

"He said the same."

"This is a good thing, right? If I'm getting close to Teagan, you can get close to Sawyer. He might tell the truth to a friend."

"He's been friendly. The guy talks nonstop and is happy to handle both sides of the conversation. He told me about his supposed time at home the entire way to football. If I'm lucky, he'll talk himself into a contradiction and prove he wasn't where he said he was."

"What are you two whispering about?"

"Nothing, Mom. Just school stuff."

Maverick ducked out and climbed in the back. I met his gaze in the rearview mirror. A silent agreement passed between us to pick this up later. My mom didn't need to know that she sent me to another school plagued by twisted secrets.

MAVERICK

"Cyd, you work on the build while I get the bugs out of the code. The crane should have been operational two days ago."

"Yes, sir, president, sir."

I snorted. "Maverick works just fine."

My vice president winked, snatched a tool off my station, and wandered over to the gears, wires, and metal on its way to becoming a first-place champion.

I liked Cydney—despite her declaring me her nemesis when we first met. I walked in as the son of Marcus Beaumont, and the advisor let me on the team without putting me through the initiation. Cydney pelted me with questions the first few weeks, testing my knowledge and growing more irritated/impressed when she couldn't trip me up. I can't say that she liked my being chosen for president over her, but we settled into an easy rhythm since the start of summer.

I sat down at my laptop, scrutinizing where we went wrong. A shadow fell over me.

"How long you been doing this?"

"Twelve seconds," I replied without looking up.

Sawyer laughed. "I meant writing code. Working with computers."

"Took apart my first one when I was five."

Sawyer pulled up a chair. Not sure what part of my hunched shoulders and tapping fingers signaled that I was interested in company. They must have because he got comfortable.

A month into summer vacation and Sawyer was entrenched in my robotics team, football buddies, and, at times it felt like, my life. I saw him three times a week and extra if Cydney, Davis, and the other guys invited us out on weekends. The worst part was he wasn't that bad of a guy.

He made everyone laugh. Offered to pay for lunch when we ran late. And he pulled his own weight on the team. If he wasn't holding up the lie that made my friend and girlfriend look like nutcases, I'd like the guy.

I have to remember he's the victim. Even if he doesn't look, sound, or act like it.

"Makes sense when you have a dad like Marcus Beaumont. I mean, when your father names the company after you, it's pretty clear what path he wants you to take."

"It wasn't like that," I found myself saying, fingers still tip-tapping away. "My dad never put pressure on me. He shared what he loved with me and it turned out that I loved it too. But he's told me more times than I can count that if I didn't want the company, he'd support my decision."

"Must be nice," he said softly. "There's only ever been one path for me."

"Yeah?" I glanced up. "What path would that be?"

He lifted a shoulder. "Straight-As. Football. Somerset. Serving my country. A house on a corner street with a wife and three kids just like my dad. It didn't occur to me that I could choose another path. He certainly never made it seem like I had a choice."

"Rough," I muttered. "If all of that isn't what you want, then what is?"

Sawyer's gaze was focused somewhere over my head. He spoke to the wall rather than me. "I was always good with computers too. Working for a start-up and making things happen with my own hands. That's what I want. And the wife and kids doesn't sound so bad if that wife is Teagan."

Sawyer shook himself, eyes landing on me. "But it is what it is. We take the cards we're dealt in life."

"I've never liked that saying." I finally looked up from the laptop. "Makes it sound like we don't have control over our destiny. Teagan appears to like you just fine and there are many ways to serve your country. That start-up could be your way. It's only giving up when you give in."

He cracked a smile. "You don't say much, but when you do, you say it all." Sawyer clapped my shoulder. "It'll never be that simple for me, and yet you're right, giving in is giving up."

"Help Cyd adjust the crane," I said, cutting our feel-good moment short. "I think I've found the issue with the code. It should work now."

Sawyer rapped the desk and took off, bending over the robot with Cydney and Davis. The room collectively held their breath as I joined them and put my fix to work. We stared at the robot like parents waiting for their kid's first step. I hit enter and—

"Whoo!"

The crane rose on oiled gears, turning this way and that. I fought a smile as Cydney socked my shoulder and Sawyer threw his arm around me

"Hot damn," Cydney cried. "We might actually get our summer back."

"We're not finished yet," I warned. "We have to test it in the obstacle course and make sure it's not top-heavy."

"We can do that tomorrow," Sawyer said. "We've been at this for hours and finally made progress. Now let's make progress on filling our stomachs. Manzoni's, anyone?" He got a yes from the whole team. "What do you say, Maverick? Lunch on me."

We have been at this since ten and Cydney finished my stash of protein bars yesterday.

"All right. Manzoni's it is, but it's on me. You guys have been great coming in on your time off. You can clean out the menu if you want."

"Oh, I want," said Cydney, bumping my shoulder. "I'm eating all the breadsticks they have in the place."

We packed it up, put away our tools, laptops, and soon-to-be winning robot, and I locked our club room. Somerset had the facilities to give the robotics team their own space and budget. That wouldn't change as long as we continued to bring in the gold.

Which we will.

Our group split apart in the lobby, each of us heading to our parking lots. Sawyer and I ended up going in the same direction, crossing the quad for the lot nearest the east entrance. He might have struck up a conversation if my phone didn't ring five minutes in.

"Hey, baby, where are you? I'm on my way to pick Adam up from his playdate, and then I was planning to come home and have my way with you."

"I'm fully on board with that plan. I'm taking the team to Manzoni's, but I should be home in a couple of hours."

"Manzoni's? Ooh, I love their breadsticks," said Val. "Mind if we crash the party?"

"Course not. You're closer, so you might get there before me. If you do, grab a table for ten."

"Will do. Love you."

"Love you too."

"Valentina joining us?" Sawyer asked as I hung up.

"Yes."

"It'll be cool to talk to her. Get to know her better. Teagan says she's a great president, and she was elected as a sophomore, so she has to be something."

"She is that." I pulled ahead, waving over my shoulder.

Manzoni's was on the other side of town. A good half an hour drive from campus and their food was worth every mile. They had the upper-class feel that Evergreen denizens expected. Flickering candles on the table. Starched white linen tablecloths and soft, upholstered seats. The family-friendly, laid-back servers, and a steady crowd of younger patrons made the restaurant a comfortable place to hang out.

I was the first of my group to arrive. Pulling into the spot next to Val's car, I killed the engine, climbed out, and strode inside without waiting for the others. Val waved me over from a large corner booth in the back.

Adam sat on her lap, scribbling in his coloring book with his tongue poking out—reminiscent of Val when she was intently working on something.

I sat down and gifted Val a kiss and Adam a ruffle of his hair, pulling a giggle out of him.

"Hi, Daddy," he cried. "I'm drawing you a robot. It's your favorite."

Sure enough the half-colored picture in his book was of a smiling robot with hearts for eyes and waving pinchers for hands.

"Thank you, little man." I plopped him on my lap. "This weekend, I'll start teaching you how to build a real robot."

"Isn't he too young for that?" Val asked over his cheers. Her beautiful face couldn't be marred by the worry lines wrinkling her brow. "All those tools you use are dangerous."

"They have building kits for young kids. And I'll be there with him." I found her hand under the table. "Or we could. How about a family project? One for each of us."

"I'd love that," she murmured. Val leaned in, pressing a kiss to my lips that communicated her feelings in more than words.

"Aww. You guys are such a cute family." Cydney slid in on the other side of the booth.

"We are, aren't we?" Val teased. The ladies hugged, lapsing into a conversation about their weekends. Cydney took her time warming up to me, but she fell for Val within ten minutes of meeting her.

It didn't take long for the others to arrive. We piled in, me and Sawyer at the end of the half circle and the others fanned out around us. The waiter arrived with our menus. I held it up before me and Adam and rested my chin on his curls.

"What are you in the mood for, Adam? You can have anything you want."

"Ummm. I want"—he pointed at a random item—"this one."

I lifted a brow. "A strawberry pisco sour? I admire your taste in drinks, my man, but I thought you were laying off the sauce! You've come so far."

Adam clapped his hand over his mouth, trapping in his giggles.

"Remember those days—passed out in the sandbox. You've fought so hard for your sobriety, don't give up on—"

Val's swat on the shoulder cut my pleas short. Adam and my team were cracking up. She was having another reaction.

"Don't even joke about that," she said to me. Val popped a kiss on Adam's cheek. "No pisco sours for you, my baby. You can have the cheese ravioli and a small soda. Sound yummy?"

"Yes."

"Good choice."

A voice drew our eyes up.

"I think I'll have cheese ravioli too."

I felt Val stiffening beside me. Aiden flashed us a huge grin as he walked up to our table and sat down next to Sawyer, bold as shit.

"What are you—"

"Hope you don't mind, Rick," Sawyer cut in. "Since we're all just hanging out, I invited Aiden to join us."

Schooling my face, I scrutinized him behind hooded eyes, looking for a trace of fear, tension, anxiety. Something you'd see when the guy who lured you to a van to be snatched in the middle of the night rolled up on you.

Aiden turned that grin on me. "You don't have to pay for me. I'll cover myself. I just had to get out of the Sam house. It's weird with no one there."

Val and I shared a silent communication. How thrilled she was to see him was clear in her eyes. All the same, she gave me an imperceptible nod.

Let him join us.

"You're staying on campus?" Val asked.

"Yeah. Coach is friends with a professional football trainer. He offered a few guys the chance to spend the summer training with him. I couldn't pass that up." Aiden bent over, crossing his arms on the table, and smiling at the boy on my lap. "You must be Adam. Nice to meet you. I'm Aiden."

He put out his hand and Adam shook it in his tiny grip. "Hi, Aiden."

Aiden pulled a face. "How old are you? Thirty? Fifty years old?"

"No," Adam cried, howling. He threw up his fingers. "I'm six."

"Six? Wow. If you're six, then you're plenty old enough to..." Aiden fished something out of his pocket. "Learn a magic trick."

A coin wedged between Aiden's pointer and middle fingers. Before his eyes, he flashed his hands and the coin disappeared. I couldn't see Adam's face but I sensed his mouth was hanging open. When Aiden reached over and pulled the coin out of Adam's ear, his jaw was on the floor.

"Wow!" Adam bounced on my lap, clapping as Aiden bowed. "Teach me, teach me!"

"Is that okay, Val?" Aiden asked.

Val looked from Aiden to Adam, clearly torn. She had the fiercest protective streak I'd ever seen and my mother wouldn't let me sleep over my friend's house until she'd done background checks on the entire family.

"Alright," she finally said. "That's fine."

Adam hopped off and went to Aiden. His eyes were big as saucers as Aiden showed him the trick again.

"Val," Cydney spoke up. "I don't think I ever got the story of how you guys met."

"Maverick and I went to the same high school." Valentina answered without taking her eyes off Adam and the Sams' ever-smiling, always-deceitful president. "We were paired together for an art project." She squeezed my thigh. "The painting he did of me was gorgeous. One of my man's many talents."

"Computer genius. Footballer and artist," Davis said. "Tell me you composed a concerto when you were nine and I'll just crawl under the table and die now."

"No." I shook my head. "I was ten."

They laughed.

"I can back up his skills on the field," Sawyer said. "Can't stop Rick once he takes off."

"Yeah?" Aiden chanced a look at us while Adam tried to get the quarter from his ear. "You should join us for a game sometime. Drop in on practice."

"Your coach would be cool with that?"

"An unofficial practice, of course. When we're having a friendly game. You free Friday at three?"

"No, I'm not," I replied. "Thanks for the invite, though. Maybe some other time."

"Tuesday. We can meet up after robotics. You too, Sawyer."

"I can do Tuesday," Sawyer said.

They both looked at me, waiting for my answer.

"Sure," I heard myself say. "Tuesday is good."

Aiden went back to Adam, slowing down the trick so he could try again. Val put her lips to my ear.

"Are you sure, baby? Don't feel like you have to hang out with them for me."

Grasping her hand, I dropped kisses on her knuckles. "I'd do anything for you. By now, we're in this together."

I didn't say more than that. She knew what I meant.

The waiter returned carrying his notepad. Valentina called for Adam, looking much happier at holding him and putting distance between him and Aiden again.

"Tuesday," Aiden said to me. "Better come to play, Beaumont. This isn't flag football on the quad."

I smirked. "Don't worry about me. I always come to play."

SAWYER BARRELED THROUGH his opponents like a freight train, coming for me head-on. I faked right as he dove, doubled back, and took off across the field.

Aiden's breath was on my neck. The huffing and puffing of his fight to gain on me caused gale-force winds. I picked up speed. The touchdown was within my grasp as sure as the football digging into my rib cage.

There was coding. The heady knowledge that I could create something. Move something. Change something with my mind and a string of ones and zeros. There was chasing my dogs through the grass. Val's smile when I woke her with a kiss and a steaming cup of tea. Playing no-stakes poker with the guys.

There was all of that... and then there was that moment as I flew over the field with hulking masses on my tail and the goal in my sights. That's the moment when I knew I was untouchable. No one and nothing could hurt me again.

Aiden dove.

I sailed over his grasping arms and touched down in the end zone, howling my victory. I relished the feeling in the time it took for my new team to descend, grabbing me and hoisting me in the air.

"Holy shit, Aiden," one of the guys said. "How is he not on the team?"

Aiden peeled off his helmet. Sweat plastered his hair to his face and flecks of dirt dotted his cheeks. He lost and had the mud on his face to prove it. Still, he grinned.

"I don't know how we missed you, Maverick Beaumont, but you're with us now."

VALENTINA

"Whoo!"

Adam and I hollered and cheered our heads off from the stands. I had a free afternoon and watching Maverick run around in a football uniform was up there with my top favorite things. There was also the matter of keeping an eye on Aiden-freaking-Connelly.

"Mommy, will I play football like Daddy?"

"If you want to," I said. "Or you could be my bubble boy. Stay wrapped up in plastic and never do anything remotely dangerous until ten years after Mommy is gone."

"No," he said, laughing.

"Yeah, I didn't think you'd go for that either."

My phone buzzed in Adam's hands. I let him film the video of Maverick playing. One of the many ways he was proving he was a big boy now.

"Is it Fia?" he asked. "Are we going to see Cinnamon?"

A glance at the screen crumpled my brows. "No, it's not Sofia."

I answered the phone and spoke to the person I never expected to call me.

"Teagan?"

"Hey, Val." Her cheery voice rang through bright and clear. "Is this a good time?"

"Yes, it's fine."

I plugged Teagan's number into my phone along with all of the sisters just in case there was an emergency at the house. It was rare for any of the girls to use it—let alone the one still fervently denying there was more behind her absence from the house.

"Is something wrong?"

"No," she said. "The opposite, in fact. You know there are only three girls who stayed in the house for the summer. Jade is here to keep things running, but it's crazy boring being in this big place without everyone.

You live nearby and Sawyer says you come to campus all the time with your boyfriend. I was thinking—if you had time—that it would be cool if we organized some activities for the four of us.

"Doesn't have to be intense like in fall and spring. We could hit the gym together. Do some movie nights. Have dinner— And you're totally thinking why in the hell would I give up my vacation, aren't you?" She laughed. "I'm sorry. I shouldn't be bugging you."

"No, no, no," I said quickly. "What I'm actually thinking is what a great idea that is. You guys must be numbed out of your skulls just sitting around when we're used to doing activities three or four times a week. Of course I wouldn't mind getting together for dinner or grabbing a movie."

"Really? Awesome. She said yes, guys." The last part was clearly not for me. "You're on campus now for the football game, right? The girls and I are going for cupcakes. Meet us and we can strategize."

"I've got my son with me." I winked at Adam. "He's not about to say no to cupcakes, but I can't stay long. He's got a date with Cinnamon."

Teagan chuckled. "I won't pretend I know what that means. Can't wait to see him either way."

I hung up and bent to gather Adam's things. "We're going to say bye to Daddy and then we're getting cupcakes. Sound good?"

I didn't even have to ask. Squealing, Adam took off running, leaving me standing there with his backpack held up for him to put on, and raced down the bleachers to get the goodbyes over with so he could jump to the cupcakes.

Maverick stood by the water cooler with a bunch of guys, laughing and trading conversation easily enough that I knew he was in his element. Maverick wasn't what you'd call shy. He didn't avoid people, crowds, leadership, or attention.

It was more that he knew himself. He had his friends, his love, his family, and his talents. Everything and everyone that made him happy was within reach. Why seek more?

He didn't pursue college ball because his namesake and legacy, Maverick Technologies, was his future and he was content with that.

Aiden gripped his shoulder, pounding his chest with the other hand, and beaming as I caught the tail end of his praise. Maverick's pleased acceptance shone in his eyes.

Or was he content?

"Daddy." Adam launched at Maverick and was caught before he hit the ground. "You were so cool."

"Thanks, little man. I won so that I could give you this." Maverick tossed him the game ball. Adam clutched it like it was ice cream, monster trucks, and staying up past his bedtime all rolled in one.

I slid in next to them, engulfed in the thick scent of sweat, dirt, and raspberry Gatorade, and hugged my boys.

Aiden downed the last of his drink, tossed it at the trash, and thumped Maverick's chest. "It's not too late for you to join. Come to the next official practice and let Coach see you on the field. Talent recognizes talent."

"I've got too much going on to commit to the team," Maverick replied.

I listened close for a trace of regret.

"This was fun, though."

Aiden shook his head. "At least come out and practice with us sometime. Next week."

"Text me. I'll let you know."

My brows shot up an inch. When did they exchange numbers? Was this in an effort to get close to Aiden or did Maverick truly want to play football with this guy?

I asked as soon as the guys were out of earshot.

"The former," he said. "You said last year that you had to do this alone because none of us had a reason to get close to Aiden. Now I do." Maverick shifted Adam to the other hip and slipped his fingers through mine. We set off for the locker room at a slower pace. "I'm not about to join the football team but meeting up for a few games will give me an excuse to get to know the guy and what he's about. I'm especially interested in just how much he knows about computers."

I glanced at Adam and carefully chose my words. "The pretense is gone, Maverick. He knows we're onto him. He knows that we—we as in you—looked him up in freshman year, and he knows that I don't trust him and that my boyfriends aren't about to trust him either."

"There isn't another way, Val. He's got one more year on this campus and we're no closer to figuring out why he's stalking his brothers or why he had one kidnapped. I can't pass up a chance to get close to the guy when he's dangling it in my face."

"I don't like this." I kissed his cheek. "Promise me you'll be careful. Play ball with him in front of witnesses. Get lunch in crowded restaurants. If he asks you to run to the van to grab a keg, say no."

Maverick threw me a lopsided smile. "It's not so easy to haul me around, Val."

Humming, I said, "I can attest to that. It's like sleeping under a two-ton boulder when you roll on top of me in the night."

"Dang. It's not that bad, is it?"

"It's not bad at all." I dropped my flirty tone. "But still, Maverick..."

"No keg runs for me. Promise."

We stopped just outside of the locker room. A chorus of slammed lockers, squeaky sneakers, and rattling pipes poured out.

Maverick put Adam on his feet. "Are you taking Adam back home or sticking around? I was thinking of swinging by my parents' place."

"Actually, we're meeting a few of the sisters at that cupcake place by the south entrance. We'll see you at home."

We kissed goodbye, and Adam and I left the stadium. The walk across campus was twenty minutes. I opted for the scenic route, pointing out a few of my favorite places to Adam.

"That's where Auntie Fia and I lay out a blanket and study on the quad," I told him. "You can claim that spot too when you go to school here."

"I'm going here too?"

"Yes, sir." Our clasped hands swung between us. "It's a local school for you, my boy, because Mommy couldn't stand it if you went out of state. Promise you'll never leave me?"

"I promise." He swore it so solemnly, I half expected him to cross his heart.

"You know, I'm going to hold you to all of these promises. Doesn't matter that you're six." I tickle-attacked him. Adam squealed and tried to run. I scooped him up, peppering his cheeks with kisses. "A promise is a promise."

"Promise is a promise," he repeated.

My face threatened to crack, my smile stretched that wide. "Why are you so cute?"

"Because you're my mommy."

Jaxson taught him that reply. It served to warm my heart every time.

"You get two cupcakes for that."

Adam was predictably thrilled.

Cupcake Queen was a recent addition to our campus. They opened shortly before school let out for the summer, and in that finals week, Sofia and I squeezed in four visits. We gave an establishment plenty of tryouts before we included it in our favorites. We were diligent like that. And Cupcake Queen quickly rose to the top.

Inside was a pink, sweet-scented haven of colorful booths, pink chandeliers, and tiny lamps overhead covered with a pink shade. Teagan and the girls occupied the booth in the middle. They munched on their cupcakes and two empty seats waited at the end for us to join.

I let Adam run to the display case. He put his face to the glass, marveling at the multitude of colors and flavors.

A server emerged from the back.

"Hi. Can I have the triple salted caramel and the churro cupcake, please? And for my sproglet"—I knelt next to Adam—"how about the funfetti and the s'mores cupcake?"

"I want that one." He tapped the glass, pointing out the ice cream sundae cupcake—so named because it was topped with a mound of buttercream shaped like a scoop of ice cream. To compound the sugar, they drizzled chocolate, covered it with sprinkles, and then graced it with a cherry.

"That is going to load you up with sugar, but I gotta say it looks good." I nodded to the server. "One of those, please, and the funfetti."

We collected our treats and carried them to the table. The girls greeted us, fussing over Adam and showering him in compliments. My son was destined to be handsome, and at this rate, he'd grow up knowing and basking in it.

Teagan and the girls hanging out for the summer semester were as different as the cupcakes they chose. I knew all of my girls, of course, but naturally I didn't get dedicated one-on-one time with all of them. Sabrina, Kendra, and Eve were among those I only spent time with during exercise and activities.

Eve was a women's studies major. Piercings in her nose, lip, and eyebrow, coupled with a height a foot taller than average, made her stand out in any crowd. Her hobbies included horseback riding, climbing, and spending all her time at her boyfriend Ben's place off campus. Those activities took her from the Sally house a fair bit.

Kendra studied cinematography and film. She was a sweetie and looked it too. She opted for Peter Pan–collar dresses, hair bows, and purple Mary Janes. Her tiny button nose and pouty lips lent her the appearance of being younger. We'd had a couple great discussions about films to show on movie nights. Otherwise, she spent a lot of time with her arty friends filming the piece that would be her senior project.

And then there was Sabrina, our lone statistics major, whose all-consuming passion to graduate top of our year, and on top of life in general, drove her to cut out all distractions. She was fit and it showed in our physical activities. Running track since middle school let her sail through workouts while I huffed and puffed beside her. She didn't date as far as I could tell and the only indulgence it seemed she allowed herself were the monthly trips to the salon to tease, blow, and style her voluminous chestnut waterfall.

Sabrina swept that waterfall over her shoulders, fanning herself with her hands. "It's steaming today. The AC must be straining."

"Oh yeah," I said. "We about melted on the stands."

"How'd the game go?" Teagan asked.

"Maverick's team won."

"Wow. Not an easy feat when going up against Aiden and Sawyer. He must be good."

"He is." I paused to wipe Adam's icing mustache. "What have you guys been up to this summer?"

"Filming my documentary," said Kendra. "Evergreen is a strange pocket of the world. An insular community that got famous in recent years for— well, you know. I've scored interviews with historians and even some of the family members involved. Most of them were only available in the summer and I couldn't pass that up."

"Double major," Sabrina threw in. "I have to do an extra summer semester if I want to graduate on time. It hasn't been so bad though. I like Somerset like this. Quieter. Relaxed. Everyone focused on what they're here to do."

I nodded. "It is nice. Sofia and I have taken to picnics on the quad. Like you said, it's much more chill these days. What about you, Eve?"

"Same for me. I'm doing an extra semester to graduate on time," she said. "And also same that there isn't much to do since all my friends left for the summer. Which brings us here, begging our prez to keep the fun going."

I laughed. "I seem to spend just as much time on campus as I did when classes are in session, so I'm down to run your lives again."

Kendra placed her hand on her chest, heaving a grand sigh of relief. "Thank you."

"I was telling the girls that we could meet up at the gym once a week," Teagan said. "And we could do the cooking thing you started where we choose a dish and make it for everyone. Full disclosure, we're voting you go first because none of us can cook and it's getting desperate."

Whatever helps me get closer to you, I thought, smiling in tune to their laughter. "Fine with me. I love cooking and this one loves being my helper." I ruffled Adam's hair. "So how about this. We keep it informal and meet up at the gym once a week. If one of us can't make it, it's cool. Same for cooking and movie night, let's arrange them for when we're all free."

"What about Thursday?" Kendra asked. "I don't have anything on that night. We could cook together."

"Okay."

"Thursday's good."

"Good for me too."

I flicked down to my son. "What do you think, Adam? Does Thursday work for your busy social schedule?"

"Yes," he said very seriously. "I want to cook with you."

"Thursday it is, guys."

We stayed for a bit longer, planning other things for us to do, and syncing our schedules. An hour later, I carried Adam to the car and he sugar-crashed in the backseat. I rode up the drive to Shea Manor and parked in our second six-car garage.

Adam snoozed on my shoulder as I brought him inside and climbed the stairs to his bedroom. Voices floated out of his door.

"—back wall. We've got a spare bedroom we can turn into his playroom."

"We'll ask Val what she wants to do."

"Knock knock," I said softly, stepping into the room. "What are we asking Val about?"

Caroline, Ryder, Olivia, and a complete stranger turned at my voice. The new woman was a sight to behold in red stiletto heels, a black pea coat, and a pen tucked behind her ear. I wasn't certain why this glamourous creature was in my son's room, but she stepped forward with a pleasant smile on her lips and her hand extended.

"Hello. My name is Daphne. You and this little guy must be my new clients."

"Clients?"

Caroline spoke up. "We were talking about this just the other night, Val. Adam is starting to get too big for this room, the race car bed, and building blocks wallpaper. I hired Daphne to give his space a makeover."

"We were talking about this the other night because I was *mourning* him getting too big for his room."

She patted my cheek. "Embrace it, dear. I'd have kept my Ryder a roly-poly baby if I could, but he insisted on growing up. Think of this as a fun project we can do together." Caroline pressed a soft kiss to Adam's forehead. "We'll go so he can take his nap."

Caroline, Olivia, and Daphne swept out of the room, continuing the conversation about his new playroom. I gave Ryder a look.

He smirked. "Like she said, Val. Embrace it."

"How about you embrace me. Twenty minutes. Your room."

"Now that I can do."

Exactly twenty minutes later, I was lying on Ryder, my chin propped on his bare chest and my toes tapping a rhythm on his ankles.

We often decompressed like this. Just stealing a moment out of the afternoon to talk.

A band of light streamed through the window, falling over his silver eyes. One arm draped over his forehead. The other absentmindedly trailed up and down my spine, popping goose bumps on my sensitive skin.

I stroked his jaw. "You're just too pretty, you know that? Mere mortals go about their daily lives doing the best they can, and then they see you, a deity in a pair of designer slacks, and they wonder what's the point?"

His laugh shook me. "Should I feel guilty?"

"You wouldn't even if you should."

"True." The reply would be arrogant coming from anyone else. Not Ryder Shea. "How'd the game go today?"

"Maverick killed. He did so well, Aiden tried to convince him to join the team."

"Sawyer was there too, right?"

I nodded.

"How does he act around him?" Ryder moved his arm behind his head, lifting up to look at me. "Sawyer's backing up Aiden's lies, but some animosity has to be bleeding through for the guy that had him taken."

"If it is, he's hiding it extremely well. Sawyer voluntarily invited Aiden out to eat with us the other day. If you secretly hate the guy, why let him crash in on your free time?" Something Aiden said whispered through my mind. "Aiden taunted me once. Saying it was possible that Sawyer didn't come back because he liked it where he was. Maybe Sawyer isn't acting like he hates Aiden... because he doesn't."

"I doubt he had him thrown in the back of a van and taken to a year-long bachelor party," Ryder said. "None of this makes a lick of fucking sense."

"Agreed." Scooting up, I dropped a kiss on his lips. "Sawyer is on the robotics team and Aiden is roping Maverick into football. I'm breaking my promise to forget all of this craziness too. Teagan and the other sisters staying on campus want us to hang out this summer. I can't be around her and not wonder where she truly went."

"If you're going to hang around the sorority, you need—"

"Please don't say bodyguards."

"—a security detail," he finished. "Val, you just said they're sucking you back in."

"It's four girls wanting to get together for food and Theo James movies. I don't need protection for that. And I'll let you in on a secret, I suggested martial arts training as a physical requirement so that I or one of the other girls could defend ourselves if a Leighton-double appeared to take us away. I'm not giving up on my normal summer."

"How stubborn are you going to be about this?"

"Extremely."

The corner of his mouth quirked up. "The usual, then."

I flicked his nose. "And don't have them covertly tail me or put any trackers on my phone, Ryder Shea. You don't want to get in trouble for that again."

"I promise," he said, holding up two fingers.

"You're lying through your teeth, aren't you?"

He almost lost it. "There's that stubbornness. I'm in trouble even if I agree with you."

"Chalk it up to how well I know you."

Ryder expelled a breath, his grin melting away. "I just want you safe, Val."

"I know you do," I whispered.

"If anything happens to you, Maverick, Ezra, Jaxson, and I will burn that sorority down with everyone in it. Can't have our story end with triple life sentences."

I kissed him—slow and sweet. "No, we can't have that."

"Look. We said we wanted to put this aside for the summer, so let's do it." Ryder flipped us over, laying us on our sides, and brushing his nose against mine. "Forget the Sallys. Tell me where you want to go on the surprise vacation I'm taking you on in two weeks."

"What? Are you serious?!"

"I'm told I don't joke, so I must be serious."

"Just the two of us or everyone?"

Ryder snuggled me tight to his chest. "Just the two of us. I plan on locking you inside the bedroom and not letting you out until we break the world record for chain orgasms, and to that end, don't pick a place you'll be tempted to explore. We're not doing any sightseeing."

"Unless the major sights are at the end of your cock?"

"Now you're getting it."

Giggling, I kissed his jaw and nose. "Sign me up for a cabin in the woods."

"I'll book it now."

Ryder got on his laptop.

I draped myself over his shoulder, laughing and messing around with him while we looked for a place to stay. We decided on the Kana Kura cabins in Costa Rica. Our own piece of jungle to relax, reconnect, and screw each other's brains out.

"This is how you spend a summer," I said. "It's almost time for dinner. I'll check if Adam's up and get him ready."

We kissed like we weren't about to see each other in a few minutes. Leaving his room, I poked my head into Adam's and landed on an empty bed. I went to Caroline's room to search for him and found it empty too.

He must have woken up and latched on to one of his dads. Jaxson is at work, so...

I pushed into Maverick's room and there they were. All three of them.

"We'll keep her comfy." Maverick packed more pillows around the dog. "Should be any day now."

"Why am I walking into every room today feeling like I'm missing something big?"

Maverick, Adam, and the blue heeler lifted their heads at my arrival.

"Hey, babe. I went to see Mom today and she sent me off with an extra."

I joined them at the foot of our bed. Maverick had made her a fortress of blankets and cushions. The pup dropped her head on my hand as I petted her soft, fuzzy head.

"Is she sick?"

He shook his head. "Mom's been looking after her for a friend who is out of town. Said friend never got her fixed and this little madam made a break for it several weeks ago and gave it up to whoever was offering."

"Maverick," I hissed, laughing even while I nodded at Adam. He didn't need to learn about her Jezebel-ing ways. "You're telling me she's pregnant. Ready-to-pop pregnant?"

"I was just telling Adam she should have the puppies any day now."

"I see," I said slowly. "And is she having these puppies in our bedroom?"

"'Fraid so. Mom signed up for one extra dog. Not a new mother and a litter of puppies. They're our problem now. At least until her friend gets back from vacation."

I stroked her swollen belly. Her tail wagged, basking in the attention. "What's her name?"

"Nala," said Adam. "Mommy, can we keep the puppies? Please, please, please."

"They're not ours to keep. Plus, we already have a cat."

"Cara is Cara's," he said, matter-of-fact. "The puppies will be mine."

But somehow the boys and I will be the ones taking care of them.

"We'll see." I picked him up. "Come on, baby. Let's get washed up for dinner."

We left Nala to ponder the life choices that left her spitting out puppies on a stranger's bedroom floor and went down to eat. After dinner, Ezra and I got Adam ready for bed and curled up next to him until he fell asleep.

"I hear Ryder's whisking you away to Costa Rica." Ezra shut Adam's door behind us. "I'm starting to think you and I are due for a vacation."

"I like you thinking that."

"My dad wants me to visit over winter break. Come with me. We'll get a hotel and I'll visit them during the day and explore you"—he hooked my waist and spun me into his chest—"at night."

My breath ghosted over his lips. "I hear your proposition and raise you a stopover in Paris. I've always wanted to visit during wintertime... and get frisky under a certain landmark."

His growl rumbled from the pit of his chest. "I accept your terms, Valentina Moon."

Ezra and I parted at Maverick's door. I wanted to check in with him and the newest addition to the Shea home.

Maverick was where he was most nights—sitting up in bed bent over his laptop. He was also dressed in his usual bedtime attire. Soft knit pants and a sleeveless tee that showed off what his regular clothes did little to hide, but concealed enough to be criminal. The dips and ridges of his sculpted body turned simple pajamas into sinful seduction.

My thoughts threatened to veer X-rated if it wasn't for the black and white dog chilling on his ankles.

"I don't think so, Nala. You want someone to snuggle up with, find the one that knocked you up. This man's mine."

Maverick burst out laughing. "You've got four of us. Maybe you could share just this once."

"Nope." I jumped on the bed, bouncing them both. "Where did you put her bed?"

"In the closet. It's bigger than the average two-bedroom apartment, so she'll be comfortable. With me, you, Adam, the guys, and the house-keepers running in and out of here, she needs a quiet place to be with her puppies."

"You know all about this stuff." I mimicked Nala's position, resting against his thigh. "How often does your mom stick you with pregnant dogs?"

"We had a lot of pets growing up mostly because I kept bringing home strays. We had enough room and money to take care of them, so my parents felt bad about sending them to a shelter. Even so, they made it clear whatever I brought through the door was my responsibility. Including the pregnant Labrador retriever I rescued when I was twelve."

Maverick threaded our fingers together. "It was good for me to have them. When... it was happening... there were times when my dogs were the only thing that could make me smile. When you're small and help-less, someone should be there for you."

I wasn't sure if that final comment was about the dogs or himself. I brought his hand to my lips, kissing his knuckles. Maverick didn't speak about this often and I knew he didn't want to speak about it now. I just held him in silent support as he caressed my palm.

He cleared his throat. "Anyway. Were you serious about consider-ing giving Adam one of the puppies? Depends on what the real owner wants to do with them, but it might be good for him."

I heaved a sigh. "I don't know if my pampered prince needs a cat, a horse, and a dog. Not to mention we have so much going on right now."

"If it helps, I'll pick up the slack. I miss having dogs. And cockatiels. And my turtle."

"You're working us up to the full menagerie, aren't you? The puppy is just the beginning."

"Got me all figured out."

I laughed which roused Nala and earned me a cheek-licking. "Thank you but kisses won't sway me to share my man either." I reached over and rubbed her belly all the same. "What are you working on?"

Maverick turned his laptop for me to see. The endless stream of data belonged to only one thing. Aiden's file.

"Maverick, you've been through that a dozen times."

"I check regularly to see if he's updated it. Who knows when he'll write something we can use?"

"He's too careful for that—which you know. And his updates will be more stalker data—which you also know." I swung my feet to the floor, towering over him. "You also know that we're taking a break from all things freaky, weird, and Aiden." I crossed my arms and gripped the hem of my shirt. "The penalty for this is clear."

Maverick tensed. Every muscle of his hard body tightened beneath those innocent pajamas. "If I have to be punished, then I have to be punished."

I slipped my blouse over my head, tossing it on top of his. "I'm starting to think you're doing this on purpose because you know the result."

Licking his lips, glazed eyes followed my slow path to the button on my jeans. "A guy's got to get it any way he can. I'm no better than the deadbeat that got Nala in trouble."

"You're way better than that deadbeat." My zipper made the most satisfying sound splitting the metal apart and revealing the lacy treat underneath. "I'm not letting you get away."

Maverick reached for me. I smoothly slid away.

"Uh-uh." I motioned to Nala. "Gotta put the dog away before we commence to the second part of the evening."

He was up and off the bed in a flash. Gently, he lifted the dog and disappeared into the closet. I heard him murmur something that sounded suspiciously like sweet dreams. Maverick was my two-ton teddy bear and I was the one fortunate to see inside to the real him.

I stripped out of my bra and panties and draped myself on his pillows. Maverick's gaze raked me from head to toe, suffusing my flesh with heat. I loved that look. It made me powerful. Like I was a mythical beauty tantalizing him to the watery depths. Drowning in me was his one true desire.

Maverick rounded the bed, fixed on me, and then he backed away. I rose up as he moved toward the couch and took a seat. "You should draw out my punishment a little more, gorgeous." He patted his lap and the hard ridge straining in his cotton pants. "Tease me."

"Oh, yeah?" I stalked across the sheets and slid to the floor, getting on my hands and knees. "That'll really make you suffer."

"It's no more than what I deserve."

Reaching him, I gripped his ankles and trailed a slow path up his legs. Maverick opened wider for me, letting me between his legs. I didn't stop at his waistband. My hands found their way under his shirt. I followed their path, gliding over his chest, my nipples skimming over the rippling flesh and hardening to points.

I bunched up the shirt and slipped it over his head, leaving his arms trapped inside. Maverick gripped my hips and rocked me on his hardness. A breathy moan escaped my lips.

"Jaxson says you dance for him. Will you dance for me?"

I knew they traded stories.

It wasn't like it mattered. I was completely open with my guys. We didn't have secrets and that included the myriad of freaky things I got up to with them. Once I went a few rounds with my vibrator for Ezra's viewing pleasure. Ryder came in halfway through and stayed for the show.

"Only if it teaches you the error of your ways."

"I'll troll that shit's files every night," he swore. "I promise."

Laughs bubbled out of me. "In that case..."

Turning on his lap, I bent over, touching the ground, and came up slowly, hips twisting. I grabbed hold of his knees and dipped, brushing his ridge and earning a sharp intake in response. He wanted this drawn out, but the punished don't set terms and I was wet and weak-kneed for him.

I dropped down, freed him, and swallowed to the hilt, earning another satisfying grunt. His length hit the back of my throat. I hummed, knowing how much he loved that. Another win for me, Maverick ran his fingers through my hair and gripped, guiding me up and down.

I played with myself, making moans that vibrated around him, and tightened his hold on me. Still, he let me set the pace. Maverick wasn't one to push or hold down. All these years later, he was still my sweet jock handling me like porcelain.

His breathing picked up, grunts rippling heat under my flesh, telling me he was close. I pulled away with a "pop."

"Why?" he cried.

Giggling, I began backing toward the bed. "You said to tease you."

"Teasing over."

"You missed the part where you're in trouble."

Maverick vaulted off the couch. Squealing, I made a run for it and was swept off my feet almost immediately. He tossed me on the bed and then himself on top of me.

I was humming with anticipation. Maverick was my sweet, gentle one... until I pushed him over the edge and dangled him. My teasing was a game we played to let the hunter out.

Maverick flipped me onto my stomach, lifted my ass up, and pushed in with one swift move.

"Oh, yeah." I made like I was going to crawl away and he growled, coming down on me like the two-ton mass of sex, heat, and need that he was. Maverick pressed my head into the sheets, resting on me cheek to cheek. He laced our fingers together in a firm fist and pinned them to the bed. I wasn't going anywhere. "You're definitely doing this on purpose."

He chuckled. "Should I stop?"

"Gotta get it any way you can, love. Although, a tip." I pushed back, driving him deeper inside of me. "You don't have to work nearly that hard. I'm ready to go whenever you walk into a room."

"I'll keep that in mind." He nuzzled my cheek, pulling a breathy sigh from me. "I love you."

"I love—"

Maverick started pumping, slowly at first, and then picking up the pace as my moans encouraged him. There was something animalistic about him on top of me, pinning me down, groans skating over my cheek, and sweat slicking our bodies.

He couldn't get an angle to pull out too far. Instead, he drove deeper. Quicker hard thrusts that rolled my eyes into my head.

"Fucking hell, Maverick," I screamed.

"Nah, I'm fucking *you*."

My comeback strangled mid-scream. I writhed underneath him, body rocked so hard by the orgasm I nearly bucked him off. Moments later, he stiffened and spilled himself inside of me.

We collapsed in a heap on the bed.

"Stay like this." I drew our hands together beneath my head. "Please."

"Thought I was a two-ton boulder?"

"You are," I murmured, "and it makes me feel safe to know between me and the world... is you."

Chapter Four

Maverick

The room was hushed. We hung on with bated breath as Bebop lifted the square, inched toward the hoop, and... let go. It sailed through under raucous shouting more suited to the final shot of an NBA match.

Cydney hugged me, jumping up and down. Nope. This reaction was warranted. Our robot, Bebop, was finished. It sailed through the obstacle course and completed every challenge without a hitch. Not only were we locked to win the competition, but we also got our summer back.

"We're celebrating," Cydney announced. "Someone volunteer for DD because we're getting trashed."

"Slow down, VP," I said. "How about we settle for lunch on me?"

"Throw a couple beers in there and you're on."

I inclined my head. We were all over twenty-one and whoever got trashed would be thrown in an Uber. No harm, no foul. And we deserved to celebrate.

"Alcohol is on me too."

"Then I'm in."

Agreement went up around the room.

"What are we in the mood for?" I asked.

"Let's order in." Sawyer slung an arm around my shoulder. "Everyone, come to the Sam house. It's practically empty. We can eat, drink, and celebrate our impending victory."

"Two good ideas in one day, boys." Cydney smacked our biceps. "I like it. Keep 'em coming."

"Cool with you, Rick?"

I shrugged. "If it's fine with you, it's fine with me. Sure you want us trashing your house?"

"Our idea of wild is spending the summer building a robot. I'm not worried about this party getting out of hand."

My team rushed around, putting away tools, shutting down the computer, packing away the robot, and finally gathering their things and heading to the frat house. I was last to leave. I locked the door and met up with Sawyer at the elevator. We rode down in a silence that for once Sawyer didn't attempt to break.

The jury was still out on this guy. I watched him during meetings, lunch hangouts, and football. I watched him with the same intensity Aiden tracked all his brothers. If Sawyer was putting on an act, he didn't break character once.

My team burst into the Sam house like kids going into a haunted house. Equal parts excited and nervous to enter the fraternity held above the rest.

"Grab some couch, guys," Sawyer said. "I'll dig up the beers. Rick, there's a decent Chinese restaurant that delivers here. Mr. Lee throws in free egg rolls if we spend more than fifty dollars."

"Good tip." I raised my voice. "Guys, want Chinese?"

"Yes!"

"Hunan chicken, please."

"Give me pork fried rice."

"Chinese it is," I said to myself.

I ventured deeper into the fraternity, on the heels of Sawyer. I'd been here before. A lifetime ago for the Halloween party that arrived early. The very night Sawyer was taken.

Nu Alpha Theta was exactly how I remembered it. Spotlessly clean not just for a house full of college dudes. It bordered on germaphobesterile. An oppressive silence clung to me as I left the crowded living room behind, and turning for the kitchen, I spotted the door that led to the basement.

If Aiden was holding a few frat guys against their will, no one would hear their calls for help down there. Not in this big, empty house.

I shook the thought loose. Valentina and Ezra have been down there. As far as we knew, the locked basement was exactly what he said it was, as well as the hidden file revealing nothing we could use.

Every door we kicked down turned up little on the other side. When will Aiden Connelly run out of lives?

"Rick? Rick."

I had stopped in the entrance to the kitchen, staring off down the hall.

"You okay, man?"

"Yep. Just flicking through the endless possibilities for summer vacation now that I have my life back." I stepped into their equally pristine kitchen and pulled up a stool at the island. "My girlfriend left for Costa Rica this morning. I might tackle a few other projects that've been sitting on my desk."

"Nah, Rick." Sawyer snagged a menu off the fridge. Grabbing the chair next to me, he handed it over. "Your first thought can't be to do more work. I won't allow it."

"You won't allow it?" I repeated, amused.

"You're so serious all the time. I get it. You're in a relationship. You've got a kid and a company to take over. But you are allowed to have fun." A slow grin spread across his face, revealing a chipped canine I hadn't noticed before. "Don't tell anyone about this, but the guys and I host a poker night most weekends." He nudged my arm. "We've got one on tonight. You should come."

"Who is we?"

"Me, Aiden, Rowen, Winston, Nasir, and Hayes. We're stuck on campus for the summer. Might as well make the most of it."

"I don't know."

"Just come and check it out." His smile was easy and open. "It's a friendly game. We don't play for high stakes. Eight o'clock. Join us."

"I've got a dog and seven puppies I'm looking after."

"Will something happen to them if you're gone for a few hours?" He laughed. "Stop making excuses and live a little. Hang out with some cool guys. Listen to music. Smoke a cigar. Lose a little money. It'll be good for you."

"Cigars and poker. Just what I've been missing from my life." My voice was laced with sarcasm. A fine performance if I said so myself. It wouldn't do to seem too eager. Val was spot-on that Aiden was on to us. My only option left was to pretend we'd given up on solving the mystery. Sawyer and Teagan were back. Case closed.

"Think about it," he said.

I bobbed my head. "I'll see if I can. Have to check with Ezra, Jaxson, and Caroline. I have a kid and seven dogs. Can't dip out whenever I feel like it."

"Let me know."

He pushed back from the island and headed out. I sat there a minute, considering my next move with a Chinese menu gripped in my palm.

Val wouldn't want me to be alone with these guys. Not with so many questions still unanswered and the look in Aiden's eyes like the truth will wreck our lives.

I shifted in my seat, casting an eye for the doorway concealed behind a fridge, paint, and plaster.

But I'm going anyway. I was always good at poker.

NALA EYED US WITHOUT lifting head or paw. I couldn't be sure, but I imagined she was thinking "Help!" Seven incredibly eager puppies climbed, wriggled, and burrowed through their siblings for their dinner.

"You're doing great, Nala," I said.

"You're a good mommy," Adam threw in.

The two of us huddled over her in the closet that was now her domain. She and the puppies were comfortable in there. Fortunate because her true owner wasn't interested in cutting her vacation short and my mother was even less interested in caring for eight dogs.

Adam hugged the furry mother, gifting her a kiss on the head. "I'll take care of them."

"I'll only be gone for a few hours, but you're on duty. Check on them to make sure they're okay. When it's bedtime, turn off the lights."

"I sleep in the big bed."

I cracked a smile. Adam's fascination with our beds wasn't a surprise. Val put him to sleep in his own bed, and if he woke in the night, she came to his room and cuddled with him until he drifted off. He rarely slept in our beds which made it a task to conquer.

"That's right. Gotta be nearby if Nala needs you. My bed is all yours. Sure you're up for this?"

"Yes, Daddy. I can do it."

"All right." I hoisted him over my shoulder, carrying him out. "A big man with a big job needs a big meal."

Jaxson reclined on my pillows with two television trays and my big screen queued to play *Up*. Adam was watching the puppies and Jaxson was watching Adam.

The little boy snuggled into his other dad's side and dug into his baked macaroni and cheese. Jaxson met my gaze over his head.

"Are *you* up for this?" he asked. "Take it from the guy who fought off a psycho stalker. Stay away from Aiden Connelly and his murder basement."

"I'm not afraid of Aiden. Mostly because he can't touch me. Partly because he's smart enough to know I'd tell you all where I was going."

He cocked a brow. "Did you tell us all? Did a certain lady of ours get the call?"

"I've got to head out or I'll be late."

Jaxson caught the dodge. He laughed me out of the room.

In the garage, I bypassed my silver Audi and black BMW for my blue Benz. If I did disappear into the murder basement, witnesses were sure to remember a blue car.

I took off for campus, easing into the half an hour drive. Music blasted from the speakers, thumping a mix Val made me before she left. She was determined to update my musical tastes. The menu for the night was The 1975, My Chemical Romance, and Yellowcard. I loved her picks but I'd pretend I didn't because she was cute as hell when she ranted on my hopelessness.

I carved a familiar path through campus. Somerset University had a different appeal at night. Old-timey lamps cast an ethereal glow on the immaculate grounds. The landscaping didn't extend to Greek Row. The residents were responsible for their own upkeep and brown patches of grass and red Solo cups used as lawn decoration were the result. All except for the Sally and Sam house.

Pulling up to the curb, I parked in front of the house, peering through the window. A lone car sat in the driveway. The lights were off inside. If a bunch of guys were getting loose and letting off steam in there, they were doing it in darkness.

Or in the murder basement.

Maybe Jaxson had a point.

I got out and bounded up the stairs. I lifted my fist to knock, thought better of it, and twisted the knob. The door swung on creaky hinges, opening on a shadowed hallway.

"Hello? Sawyer?"

"Rick."

My eyes traveled up. A figure stood at the top of the stairs cloaked in gloom. It moved and then split apart. Not one figure. Two.

"Beaumont." Aiden reached the bottom of the landing and beckoned me inside. "Come on. We're downstairs."

I didn't let my confirmed suspicions show on my face. Silently, I stepped in, letting the door click shut behind me. I couldn't make out where anyone was until the basement door opened. The light illuminated the hall, and Aiden and Sawyer as they went inside.

They're playing up this creepy vibe.

Even so, I followed.

Voices floated up the stairs.

"—new guy. Can we trust him?"

"Rick's cool," I heard Sawyer reply. "Don't worry about him. He won't say anything."

The fifth step squeaked, bringing the conversation to a halt. I stepped off and got the full view of the basement I'd heard so much about. As confirmed, there was nothing to worry someone of even the most nervous disposition.

A whiteboard was pushed to the back of the room and covered with a sheet. A television was on the other side. A couch was pushed directly in front of it. The center of the room was taken up by the poker table and the six guys sitting around it. Sawyer pulled out the chair next to him.

"Rick, have a seat. Grab a scotch first. It's over there."

A glance to the side confirmed a bar top loaded down with a dozen bottles.

"I'm driving," I said simply, taking the seat.

Sawyer pointed out the guy next to me. "Rick, this is Winston Abernathy III." Winston inclined his head at me.

Choosing a name for an infant is a shot in the dark. Gracing the kid with a name that means warrior won't stop them from becoming a shaky-kneed coward who flinches when someone jumps. In Winston's case, I'm certain his parents saw into his future.

The man sitting next to me sat straight-backed, sipping three fingers of scotch. A gray dove-tail coat screamed money as loud as it did the eclectic taste born from wealth. At his throat was a purple cravat—yes, a cravat. And blue, disinterested eyes scanned me up and down. Everything the name Winston Abernathy the Third evoked was sitting next to me.

"Rick." A thick British accent poured out of his mouth. "What's your last name?"

"Beaumont."

The disinterest flickered. "As in Marcus Beaumont?"

"As in Maverick Beaumont," I corrected. "Nice to meet you."

"Likewise." Winston nodded almost imperceptibly to Sawyer. I had no clue why. "My family's done some business with yours. My father swears by your company."

"Glad to hear it."

Sawyer gestured to the next guy. "Meet Rowen Burke. Junior. Sam. And—"

"—the guy who'll be cleaning up tonight." He shook hands with me. "I hear you're some kind of genius, so this'll be doubly embarrassing for you."

I laughed. "Most rumors are greatly exaggerated. I bet your poker skills are one of them."

"I like this guy."

Rowen had the easy air that went along with his tone. A loose cotton shirt in contrast to Winston's suit. Sandy hair falling every which way. Puka shell bracelets adorning both wrists.

"My man, Hayes Benson," Sawyer continued.

The name and the scar splitting his left eyebrow triggered my memory. "Hayes Benson," I repeated. "From junior prep school?"

"That's right. Been a long time, Rick. Good to see you."

The time had been good to Hayes. I remembered a scrawny kid who hung out with only one friend and ate sushi every day for lunch. He now rivaled me in height and size. Seems his mom was onto something with the sushi. She ran a health food conglomerate and I knew for certain it was one of my father's clients.

"Good to see you too," I said, and meant it. "Wild that we've been going to the same college for two years and didn't know it."

"Let's catch up after this."

"For sure."

Sawyer gripped my shoulder, directing me to the final two guys. "Aiden you know, and this is Nasir Harb."

Nasir surveyed me with eyes eerily like Ezra's. If Winston was buttoned-up and Rowen was laid-back, he fell in the middle with the shirt, blazer, and jeans. He cut his hair close to the scalp and pierced three holes in his left ear for diamond studs and left the right untouched.

Aiden said they were all Sams. If the frat brothers fell into a "type," I couldn't see it.

"You any good?" he asked as we shook.

I lifted my shoulders. "Played with my dad growing up. Cleaned him out of Oreos."

Nasir smirked. "We play for more than cookies down here."

The way he said that scrunched my brow. "I thought this was low stakes."

"It is," said Hayes. "Ten thousand dollar buy-in. Pocket change."

"For some." I cut a look at Aiden and Sawyer. Hayes took his fish dumps in gold-plated toilets. Winston's father couldn't do business with mine unless he had a few million to throw around, and I couldn't speak to Nasir's or Rowen's wealth. One thing I did know for sure was Sawyer and Aiden did not have that kind of pocket change.

I looked into these guys and their finances more than once. Where did they get ten thousand to throw on this table?

Aiden held my look with his patented smirking glint. "In or out, Beaumont."

"I'm in."

Just like that, the game was on.

I may have undersold my experience with poker. I did play for cookies with my dad. Then we played for chores. During Evergreen we played for where we'd go on summer vacation, and after graduation, my boys and I played for cars, money, and who'd claim Val for their bed in the following weeks. (She didn't know about that last one.)

Poker was first and foremost a game played in the mind. The gift of reading people was one I perfected long ago while I spent my time listening, observing, waiting for people to show me who they truly were before I got close. Listening and observing was what you did in a round of poker.

Or at least that's how every single other game I've played in my life went down. Not this time. From the moment the first chip struck the felt, these guys hadn't shut up for a second.

"—want me to marry her," said Winston. "An arranged marriage in our day and age. Ridiculous."

"What's the duchess look like?" Rowen asked. "Uggo?"

Winston leaned back, turning his pleased expression to the ceiling. "Cornflower blue eyes. Hair like silk. An ass I'd tap on repeat—and have."

The guys hooted and hollered. They weren't so much as looking at their cards.

"So what's the problem?" Nasir spoke up. "Marriage is a business move. In your case, you've acquired a fine asset."

His tone left no imagination in what he meant by "fine" and "asset."

"She's a good fuck but why be limited to one for the rest of your life? I floated the idea of an open marriage and she threatened to cut the boys off with a rusty spoon. Needless to say, marriage talks are breaking down."

The guys laughed in his face. I admit I cracked a smile too.

Good for the duchess. Thirty minutes with Winston Abernathy III and it's obvious she deserves better.

"My parents aren't dangling picks in front of me," Rowen said, "but they made it clear I can't bring a wife home without a prenup. They're cut-off-my-inheritance serious."

"Same," Nasir said.

"Me too," echoed Hayes. "What about you, Maverick?"

What about playing the fucking game?

"Call," I said, tossing in my chips. "I don't have to worry about any of that. I'm not getting married."

"Makes sense." Sawyer raised and threw a handful in without even looking. "Val can only legally marry one of you. Keeps things equal to stay out of the wedding ring roulette."

Hayes pulled a face. "What the hell are you talking about?"

"Maverick and his friends have the same girlfriend." Aiden answered with the reply still on my tongue. "What do they call that again? Poly relationship or something."

Hayes blinked at me. "You serious?"

"Now that's the way to do it." Winston surveyed me in a whole new appreciative light. "If only I could get the duchess on board."

"The duchess might not object to being loved and worshiped by multiple partners," I said. "But it's Val and Val alone for me. Pretty sure your soon-to-be fiancée made it clear she'd expect to be your one."

"What about your friends?" Nasir asked. "Are you with them too?"

"Asking me if I'm with my boys is like asking how often I hook up with my sister. They're as close to brothers as I got."

"Brothers? Are you talking about Lennox, Shea, and Van Zandt?" Hayes asked. "I remember you guys used to be tight."

"Still are."

"Sooo... if I'm getting this straight," Rowen drew out, "you have one girlfriend, and your girlfriend has four boyfriends."

"And we have a son, cat, possible puppy, and a home in the Estates. Any more questions?"

The guys traded looks, ranging from astonished to uninterested—Aiden and Sawyer—and said nothing.

"Looks like I finally shut the noise down," I said, grinning away. "Now we can play some poker."

"In that case," said Aiden, "all in."

The guys stopped nattering for a solid stretch and played, contributing to the growing pile of chips in front of me.

Rowen finally shoved from the table. "Let's take a break."

The others were up on the last word. Clearly, they were cool to stop losing money to me.

"Surprised you're not three hundred pounds and choking on diabetes," Nasir said to me. We followed the others to the bar.

"What?"

"With all the Oreos you've skimmed off unlucky saps over the years."

I barked a laugh. "The weight couldn't keep up with my growth spurt, and now I skim pocket change from unlucky saps."

"You're not so bad, Beaumont." Rowen crossed his legs at the ankles, leaning against the barstool.

"Told you guys." Sawyer shot me a look of approval that, again, I didn't understand.

"Slow down," Winston said. "The real measure of a man is how well he can handle his scotch. Give this a taste, Ricky."

His fingers obscured the label. Winston poured me a generous helping and passed it over with a look in his russet eyes that he truly was seeking my measure.

I accepted, eyes locked on him, and chanced a sip. The Scottish whiskey burned a sharp and smoky trail down my throat. I hummed in pleasure. "Ten-year Laphroaig. Personal favorite of mine."

Winston's smile came slow, but it came all the same. "I'm a Balvenie man myself, but I respect your style."

Aiden moved in between us, snagging the Laphroaig as Winston went to pour some more. "Do you respect him enough to let him settle our argument?"

"Not this again," Hayes groaned. "You both made good points."

"And we're evenly split on who made the best," Aiden said. "Maverick makes an odd number. Whoever he agrees with, wins."

The guys passed glances around each other, and then at me. I weathered their scrutiny in stride. Whatever this was, they'd get to the punchline eventually.

"Okay," Winston finally said. "Maverick decides."

"I decide what?"

"Winston and I are locked in an argument on the function of laws," Aiden stated. "It came up in his textbook and our discussion spiraled like everything does with this fucker."

"It's true," Winston added.

"Hear us both out and tell us who has the better argument. You'll help us settle a bet."

"I can do that."

"Sweet. So, I say that laws exist merely to restrict social behavior." Aiden crossed the room and retook his chair. "What one person or people can do to another person. In their essence, every law was created to control people and that will always be their function. They will change only as we, and the way we treat each other, change."

I nodded, turning over his argument. "All right. Winston?"

"I say his notion is inaccurate from top to bottom. Laws don't exist merely for people-to-people behaviors. There are laws for animal welfare and cruelty. Laws protecting buildings, trees, or where you can stamp your foot in the forest in case you come down on some rapidly disappearing fauna. Laws exist to restrict our behavior, certainly, but not solely in regard to how we interact with each other."

"Lay your arms down, gentlemen," Hayes joked. "Maverick, deliver the verdict."

I took my time considering both their points. I had to agree each of their arguments were solid, but, in the end, only one truly expressed the reason for laws.

"I have to say... I agree with Aiden."

Aiden smacked the table. "You see? Tell him why, my friend."

"Yes." Winston reclaimed his seat. "Why?"

"While it's true that laws don't merely restrict our actions against people, the effect on other people is still the basis for every law made to protect objects, plants, or animals. For example, it's the horror others felt when they witnessed a man beating his dog or starving his horse that pushed them to demand laws against animal cruelty.

"Strange as it is to admit, it's not really about that animal's welfare so much as it is about the voices speaking up *for* their welfare, and the growing understanding we've accepted as a society, in the vileness of the act. The proof is in the fact that we can be charged for animal cruelty, but not for carving up an animal and eating its meat.

"One act is viewed by the majority as wrong while the other is not. Whereas I'm sure Bambi would vote for neither. Laws are only about people. What horrifies us. What goes against our interests. What hurts us and the things we care about. As Aiden said, it's all about social behavior."

A thick silence descended on the room. Absolute for our position underground. The only thing that could be heard was the screaming smugness on Aiden's face.

"I couldn't have said it better myself. Boys?"

Nasir blew out a breath. "Rick's argument is sound. Aiden wins. Winston, hand over the keys."

The cravat-wearing Brit swore under his breath as he dug in his pocket.

"Keys?" I spoke up. "Keys to what?"

"My Jag. And you're giving me a ride home, mate," he said to my openly stunned expression. "We're discussing your theory further."

"Don't bother," Aiden said. "You lost. The car is mine."

"Hold up," I cried. "Dropping ten grand on the poker table is one thing. But did you seriously bet your car on the winner of an offhand thought you got out of a textbook?"

Winston shrugged. "I've got three others."

Like that's the fucking point.

"It's all fun between friends," Sawyer cut in. He raised his brows. "Which *we* are, right? Friends."

"Slow down," I said mildly. "I'm not that easy."

The group found that amusing.

"We try to do this every week," Hayes said. "You should join us." He spoke in my direction but I had a feeling the statement was for the room.

Winston confirmed the feeling, replying, "Fine. He's a decent bloke. Let him in."

Nods went around the table.

"What do you say, Rick?" Sawyer asked. "Will we see you next week?"

My muscles moved of their own accord—contracting and loosening, moving my head up and down.

"See you next week."

WINSTON MADE GOOD ON his threat to climb into my car.

I drove him out to the beach, dropping him at his family's third home, and his sole home while he went to Somerset. The entire drive we talked laws, government, his life in England, and then a dip into our favorite television shows. Turns out he wasn't that bad of a guy when he wasn't waxing poetic about the tight pussies of his conquests.

It was almost one in the morning by the time I crawled home, dragging myself upstairs. I nearly forgot I promised Adam my bed until two mounds—one big, one small—greeted me. I didn't have the heart to carry him to his room and Jaxson was liable to take a swing if I woke him from a deep sleep. The guy got so little of that these days.

I changed, brushed my teeth, and hit my pillow face-first. We were having a sleepover and that was that.

Tonight was strange.

The thought floated on the edge of sleep, coaxing me to chase it, catch it, examine it. The poker game was odd for the reason that it was so... normal. A couple of guys drinking, talking, and shooting the shit. No part of it could be classed as suspicious. Although, betting your car to win an argument was hardcore.

Sawyer, Aiden, and the guys want me in their group, so I'll play. I'll do whatever it takes to...

"ADORABLE, AREN'T THEY?"

A dry voice knocked on my consciousness, tugging me out of sleep.

"Aww. Look at my boys."

And that voice peeled my eyes open. "Val?"

"Hi, love." Val beamed at me through the screen. "Wild night last night?"

I pushed myself up, nearly bumping into the tablet. Ezra kindly held her up higher.

Adam was splayed out next to me and on his side was Jaxson. I guess we did make a cute sight.

As does the girl I'm looking at.

Valentina looked to be reclining on a white chaise. Over her head, a canopy of lush, vibrant jungle served as her backdrop.

"How's Adam? How are the puppies? How are you?"

"Adam got to babysit and sleep in the big bed, so life is good in his world. The puppies are great and I... have a lot to tell you when you get back."

"Oh? Is now not a good time?"

I shook my head. "I want you to enjoy your vacation. It can wait."

"Okay, if you're sure," she pressed.

"I'm sure."

"Then we'll pick it up when I get back. Do you mind waking up my baby and my favorite bad boy producer? My favorite grumpy CEO says I have five minutes left."

Ryder's voice came through the speakers. "Tick, tick, tick."

"Sure."

I got the boys up and they said their greetings to Val.

With my robotics duties out of the way, I skipped out on a reason to go to campus except for football games with my intramural team and even that was canceled for the week, owing to two guys getting sick and the third heading up to Wisconsin to visit his mother. I was free to build a robot with Adam, race ATVs on the back roads with Jaxson, and let my mother guilt me into having dinner with her and Dad every other night. I even got some time in with Olivia.

"Teddy," she declared. She snuggled the little black and white pup licking her cheek. "He's sweet and cuddly like a teddy bear. It fits."

"We shouldn't name them." Olivia and I sat in the closet, giving the puppies attention while Ezra and Adam took Mom outside for a break. "They're not ours."

"If an animal spits out babies in your closet, they're yours. The owner wants to say something about it, their ass should be here."

I chuckled. Olivia was Valentina in every way. Or it was more accurate to say Valentina was like Olivia.

"We can't keep calling them 'the puppies.' Come on." She reached in the basket and pulled out one of the two girls. "What should we name her?"

"Well, she's a fierce one. She'd knock her own brother down and step on his head to get to that nipple. A girl like that should be called... Pepper."

"Pepper. I like it. Now you're getting into it." She picked up one of the boys. "And him?"

"Doc," I stated. "Because of his dopey face."

Olivia groaned. "And just like that, you're off naming duty. I'll handle it from here."

"What'd I do?" I cried, cracking up. "Doc is a solid name."

My phone buzzed in my pocket.

"This sweet boy's name is Milo"—she fixed me with a look—"and don't let me catch you calling him anything else."

I threw my hands up in surrender, phone and all. "Milo it is." I put the cell to my ear. "Hello?"

"Hey, Rick."

"Sawyer. What's up?"

"You still coming tonight?"

"Yeah. Why?"

"No reason. It's just... it's good."

My brows crept together. "What's good?"

"Having seven. See you at nine."

The click sounded in my ear, cutting off my chance to ask what the hell he meant. I pulled the cell away and stared at it in confusion like its black screen had answers for me.

"Maverick." Olivia broke into my thoughts. "Meet Pepper, Milo, Teddy, Dixie, Chester, Blue, and Romeo."

"Really?" I lifted the now-named Dixie and let her nibble on my chin. "I was thinking Sarah Jessica Barker. Or how about Virginia Woof?"

"You have now lost the right to name my grandchildren."

I fell over laughing, and was immediately descended upon by the Australian cattle dog horde.

That night, I put Adam to bed in his temporary room—mine. Daphne and Caroline began renovations on his the day before. With Jaxson and Ezra getting up early to head to work, Adam was bunking with me. Naturally, he was thrilled at being near the puppies, and I loved having the little guy around. We stayed up watching movies and eating ice cream in bed like I used to do with my dad. Also like my dad, I made him swear to keep our sugar-binge sessions a secret from Val.

Only when he was asleep did I get dressed and leave for the poker game. Jaxson called out to me as I climbed off the bottom step.

"Yo, Rick." He emerged from the living room. "Seriously, you're going to this thing again?"

"Yes, I'm going. I can't figure out what Aiden's about from the other side of campus."

He carded his fingers through his hair, somehow not messing it up. "Listen. I've been thinking. Do we need to know what he's about? Sawyer Burn wasn't chopped into pieces and scattered in the ocean like chum. He's fine. That Teagan girl is fine. Leighton Lewis—dead or alive—isn't coming back. Logan is dead. We caught the person who ran Valentina off the road. Aiden obviously didn't hurt those guys, he didn't hurt Val, and we can't prove he's hurt anyone else. Why can't we just let this one go?"

Stiffening, my grip tightened on the banister. "Because the last time we sensed something was wrong, we put our heads down, pretended everything was normal while deep down a thick rope of fear strangled us. All of us. The entire town."

"It's not like the academy."

"It's exactly like the academy," I shot back. "Someone should have put a stop to that shit a long time ago. Instead we pretended what we couldn't see, we didn't have to face. Well, I see Aiden Connelly. I see through his smug-ass grin and offers of friendship. He may not be a serial killer, but something isn't right with that guy. And that strangling fear, it chokes Val every time she sets foot in that house and wonders if there's another Leighton nearby—watching her, digging into her life, forming another group of budding sociopaths."

Jaxson crossed between me and the door. "I hear you, man. I really do. All I'm saying is what Val's been trying to tell us for months. If Leighton Lewis was a threat to her, she wouldn't have given the knife back. Whoever cleaned up that body for her might be in it with Aiden too. That's fucking serious, but it's also the cops' job to track them down. You're playing undercover hacker and putting yourself in danger for what? Connelly's too smart to slip up with you around."

"No. He's arrogant. He thinks he's always the smartest guy in the room and that's how I know he'll slip up. When he does, we'll find out the truth about Leighton Lewis, the people who've vanished from the Sams and Sallys, why he collects dossiers on his brothers, and what he knows about the people who got rid of Logan's body. The guy is right next door to Val almost every day. I won't sit around while she does what we know she will do—find the truth on her own."

"Fuck. All right." Jaxson stepped aside. "Go. Be a hero. Save our lady." His hand shot out as I took a step forward. "But if something happens. Anything. Call me. I've got your back."

"I know you do." I gripped his shoulder. "You'll run in and protect me with those noodle arms. All five foot nothing of you against the big, bad—"

"Fuck outta here," he cried, laughing. "Save your damn self."

My shoulders shook, melting away the tension. "For real, Jaxson. I wouldn't want anyone else at my back." I turned to leave. "I'll be home before midnight. Check on Adam before you go to bed."

Jaxson saw me off at the door. He ceased convincing me to stay, but his haunted gaze took up the task just fine. I understood why he embraced Val's resolution to return to normal. He just came off an intense year. Normal is what we all wanted.

We can only have that if Aiden allows it. Waiting around while he decides isn't an option.

I blasted Val's playlist on the drive. Listening to her songs made me picture her hunched over the computer, tongue poking out, and forehead wrinkled in the most adorable flipping way. It had been one week and I missed her like a limb. The scent of her sweet shampoo lingered on my pillow, and it messed me up something serious every time I climbed into bed.

The argument could be made that my boys and I were the kings of assholes. Sultans of insufferable shitheads. The pharaohs of pricks.

Ezra sized people up by what they could offer him and discarded those who came up wanting. Jaxson was as blunt as a pool noodle. He'd tell saps what he thought of them straight to their crumpling face. As for me, I didn't have many words to spare, and I gave none to people who weren't worth my time.

But none of us would ever compare to Ryder Shea.

Why?

Because he whisked Val away for two damn weeks and left us sitting here wondering why we didn't think of it first.

I spent the remainder of the ride cursing one of my closest friends in the world.

Turning onto the final street, I saw straight down the road to the once again dark house. Beside it, Sally house boasted more life. Lights flickered through the gossamer curtains of the living room. Three floors above, the outline of a woman rocked before her window.

I left behind their relative normalcy and climbed the stairs for the Sam house. The door was left open for me again. Without invitation, I let myself into the basement.

"It's Rick," someone said. "Rick! Get down here, mate. I've got more scotch for you to try."

A blanket of inky black swallowed me as I descended the stairs, flickering within it was a soft, warm glow. The boys had opted for candlelight. Why?

I stepped off the stairs and froze. Sawyer crowed about seven making perfect, but there were more than seven people here. Thirteen to be exact.

Winston leaned against the bar talking to a blonde back-of-the-head in a short pink dress. Nasir claimed the couch with two girls. His hands rested on both of their knees while theirs roamed under his shirt. Hayes posted up in the corner attempting to suck the organs out of a girl through her mouth. Aiden and the girl on his lap were at the poker table, and the final woman I recognized.

"Hi, Maverick." Teagan closed the distance, taking my hand and drawing me in. "Glad you could make it."

"Are we having a party?"

"Party?" Rowen snorted. "A party demands a hundred more people. Four times the alcohol and ten times the nudity. We're here to play poker, man."

I glanced at the girl on my arm. "Are you joining us?"

Teagan shook her head. "It's fatally boring next door. I crashed for the booze." She smirked at Sawyer. "And to see how long my man can hold out before taking me upstairs and entertaining me."

"The answer is not long." Winston rolled up on us, putting a drink in my hand. "We better get this game underway. But first"—he lifted his arm and the blonde girl magically appeared beneath it—"Rick, meet the duchess."

It was incredible to say that Winston undersold her looks. The statuesque beauty in front of me took the silky tresses and cornflower blue eyes and paired them with a mischievous twist to her lips and a firm hand on Winston's collar like she had every intention of reining him in. I was looking at a woman with means and the willingness to use them.

"Pleasure to meet you, duchess."

"Phillipa, please." She extended her hand in expectation of a kiss. "Lovely to meet you as well."

"Now that Maverick is here, we can start," Aiden announced. "Jasmine, if you don't mind."

The guys migrated to their original seats, leaving me to claim the chair between Sawyer, Winston, and Phillipa—who climbed on Winston's lap and secured his arms around her waist. I was getting the feeling the only one not interested in the arranged marriage was the overly fashionable gentleman beneath her.

Aiden zeroed in on them as well. "Winston," he said. That was it. Just his name.

"Phillipa," Winston spoke up. "Grab us a drink, would you, love?"

"What do I look like? The maid." Her voice was syrupy-sweet. Phillipa leaned in and nipped his nose. "Get it yourself."

She spun, whipping his face with her hair, and flounced off his lap. Jaw clenched, Winston watched her go and then turned to me as if to say, *see what I put up with?*

"I like her." Amusement laced my tone. "You two would make a good match."

"How would you know? We met last week."

"And yet I can already tell you need reining in."

Winston laughed. "You and every shrink Winston Abernathy Junior and his consort have sent me to."

"Guys," Aiden broke in. "Let's do this."

Winston fell silent.

He shifted a look to Nasir. "Explain the rules."

"All right. Maverick, we—"

I held up a hand. "You don't need to tell me the rules. I know how to play."

"We're playing a different game."

Looking from him to the poker table set up in front of us, I asked, "Are we?"

"It's poker," Sawyer said. "But we play it differently is what he means. You got the idea last week."

"The idea of what?" I considered myself an intelligent guy. An observant one too. But what the fuck these guys were talking about and why they kept trading looks was escaping me.

"Whoever wins tonight is asked the question and provides the answer. If the majority supports your answer, you keep your winnings. If they don't, you give it up—all of it."

I said nothing. Sawyer must have taken that to mean I needed further explanation because he launched into one.

"Like last week," he said. "The question was what is the function of laws. Aiden won the game, so Winston asked him the question. He offered up his car if he lost and would've hauled off Aiden's winnings if he won. It came down to a tie which you broke. We won't have that problem from now on."

"If I win, you ask me a question," I said slowly. "What about?"

"The guy who lost the most decides that," Nasir explained. "The question can be on any topic, but it must be one that requires actual thought. Discussion. A stance. Don't waste time with 'who is the best Powerpuff girl?'"

"Blossom," I replied without skipping a beat. "Obviously."

"Obviously." Nasir didn't miss a trick. "That's why we can skip that one."

"What's the point of this?"

"What's the point of tossing chips and cards around the table?" Aiden asked. "Poker is a game of strategy. Foresight. Anticipation. But life is a game of chance. You survive it by knowing the measure of yourself and where you stand." He spread out his hands. "We do more than mess around down here. The Sams are about more. If you don't stand by your logic and convictions to the point you'd bet everything on it, then what's the point of you?"

My expression wiped clean, giving nothing away besides a raised brow.

"Are you in or out?"

He's not asking me to sacrifice the duchess on an altar of skulls and poker chips. If I win, I get asked a question. I can handle that.

"I'm in."

Sawyer clapped me on the back, looking pleased.

If this was a test—and it was becoming clear all of this was—I seemed to be passing.

The game got underway. The guys were no less quiet the second time around.

"How do you look behind the wheel of a Jag, A?" Hayes slung a playful punch at Winston.

"Like I was born in the backseat of one."

"Probably conceived in the backseat of one," Winston shot back. "Your mum still giving it up for loose change?"

"She was," Aiden replied. "Had to quit because your mom was fighting her for johns."

"You know us Abernathys always win."

The Sams kept up the ribbing, jokes, and stories for the whole game. I let it go on unchecked. Their noise wasn't preventing me from winning. Although, I questioned if I wanted to win now that I knew the outcome.

Who thought up this question and answer game? The Sams see themselves as the best this campus has to offer. But sitting around in a grotty basement and trying to turn a poker game into some intellectual gentlemen's club? I'd say it reeked of pretention if they weren't making fart jokes and implying their mothers went legs up in the backseat for cash.

"Darling." Painted hands snaked around Winston's neck. "When will this wretched game be over?"

The girls had been drinking and talking on the couch, and the duchess was over it.

Lucky for her I was about to bring the game to an end.

"Nasir?"

Ezra-like eyes glittered as he spread out his cards. "Four aces."

The boys winced, sealing my fate.

I turned over my hand. "Straight flush."

Just like that, the hisses morphed into whoops and a few curses courtesy of Nasir.

"All right. We have our winner," said Aiden, "and our loser by the highest amount." He inclined his head next to Rowen. "What are you offering?"

"This." Rowen removed the white gold watch from his wrist.

"Hold on," I spoke up. "That watch retails at forty-two thousand dollars."

"I know. That's why I'm throwing in my canary diamond cuff links."

"You have to put up at least as much as you stand to gain," Sawyer explained.

"Right," I said. "So, he asks me a question. We both give an answer and whoever you guys agree with keeps the money. I'm the new guy. Why wouldn't you all side with your friend and cheat me out of my winnings?"

"You gotta have more faith," Aiden replied. "If you can't, then I'll tell you there's no bullshitting. We have to back up an argument with one of our own. Using details and examples of why we agree or don't, and we do that before we hear your answers. Teagan," he called.

In a blink the Sally appeared with pens and paper. She passed it around to Sawyer, Aiden, Nasir, Hayes, and Winston.

"Satisfied?" he asked.

"What if we both agree? Rowen and I may vote for the same Powerpuff girl."

"It will still come down to the better argument. But you can ask for another question if that happens."

I wasn't done yet. "And how do I know you didn't decide your answers hours before I got here? It's all well and good you writing down your answers before I give mine. Unless you already coordinated them."

"Fuck's sake." Aiden laughed. "You're a distrustful guy. Did you rub that off on Valentina or did you get it from her?"

"Leave my girlfriend out of this," I hissed.

He put up his hands. "I apologize. That was below the belt. Fair enough, you're suspicious. You don't know any of us. What do you suggest?"

"I supply a list of random questions. He chooses one and we go from there. Deal?"

Aiden swept a look around the table. The guys nodded.

"Fine."

Silence choked the room while I searched my phone for the questions. Even the ladies cut short their conversation. After a few tense minutes, I found a list of over three hundred discussion topics. No one could say I didn't give the guy plenty of options.

I passed over my phone.

"Well?" Aiden prompted.

"Some good ones," said Rowen. "Have to pick one I can defend. Give me a min— Wait. I got it." Rowen sat up straighter in his seat. "Ready, boys? Rick?"

"Ready."

"Go for it."

I dipped my chin in reply.

"Does tribalism and our habit of separating each other into groups help or hurt society?"

"Ooh. Good one," said Hayes. His pen was in his hand and flying across the page within a breath. The soft scritching of metal tip on paper *tap, tap, tapped* on my mind. Through it I held Rowen's gaze, considering what I'd say.

It was an interesting question, and I had an inkling of which way he'd lean. Wealthy. Athletic. Healthy. Attractive. Sam. Claiming membership in those groups had resulted in an enviable life for Rowen Burke. To be fair, it resulted in one for me too.

Teagan collected the others' answers and then turned on us. "First, Rowen, tell me if it helps or hurts."

"Helps."

"Maverick," she asked me. "Does it help or hurt?"

"Hurt."

"Good. We have a disagreement." She squeezed my shoulder as she sat on Sawyer's lap. "Maverick, you first."

I launched right in. "Tribalism may be ingrained in us, but it can't be denied that this habit is responsible for nearly every issue affecting our society today and societies past. Racism. Classism. Sexism. War. Genocide. Ethnic cleansing. Even something as small as which football team won or lost has resulted in fans rioting.

"This 'us' versus 'them' mentality has permeated every area of our lives and the damage has been recorded in our history books. It's something we witness every day. I recognize at its core, it's what brings us together as families, friends, and communities. Contributing and protecting each other, especially in the ages when we hunted with spears. Tribalism kept us alive to become what we are today. But when we measure the cost—weigh the genocide, chattel slavery, disenfranchisement, hate groups, terrorism, and poverty. To conclude that this has hurt society almost goes without explanation."

"Well said," Teagan praised. "Rowen. What do you got for us?"

"Ricky makes an excellent point and I don't disagree with a word of it. Tribalism is at the root of all of those issues and, of course, it has hurt our society. But despite the bad that's come with it, I say the good still outweighs, and it comes back to what Maverick said. Without those early humans coming together to feed and protect each other, Homo sapiens would've ended their short time on earth in a sabretooth's stomach.

"But tribalism isn't just community. It's the smartest minds coming together to advance science, technology, and medicine. Rarely is a discovery made in a vacuum. It's done through collaboration. We've committed terrible acts in the name of 'us' versus 'them' but we've also achieved new heights while working together to right those wrongs.

How can we say the root of all we've become is bad, when nothing good would exist without it?"

Rowen punctuated his speech with a bow, soaking in the congratulations from Teagan.

"Thank you, gentlemen," she continued. "Now I get the fun task of reading these answers. Yea or nay. Let's see who is walking away with all of it."

One by one by one, Teagan read the scribbled thoughts of my other five opponents. They each had plenty of examples in both directions, but their final decision was clear. Teagan announced the winner to applause from everyone in the room. Rowen and I stood up to shake.

"Does this mean your little game is over?" asked Phillipa. She sidled into Winston's arm. "I believe I'm owed a lot more attention than you've been giving me."

"You're going to get more attention than you can stand." Winston lifted a squealing Phillipa and tossed her on the table. He whipped her dress over her head with a speed that rivaled roadrunner, and flung it on the tower of chips.

I sprung back mid-shake and nearly slipped on one. My first instinct to rip the manhandling asshole off of her died in the fiery heat of her moan. Phillipa undid her own bra and tossed it in the direction of her dress.

"Finally." The other girls slinked off the couch, rising up to meet the boys coming for them. In Sawyer's case, Teagan swung around, straddled him, and began making quick work of his shirt and belt.

And finally I understand what these guys are about.

I hit the bottom step of the staircase as Winston's pants hit the floor.

"Leaving?" Sawyer asked.

"Yes."

"Course you are." Aiden carried his naked date to the pool table. "Committed relationship. A kid, cat, and possible dog. This part isn't for you, Ricky. But I like you." He tried to point at me and his date snagged his hand and put it between her legs. "You're in, man. See you next wee—"

That's all he got out before she captured his lips. I got the gist.

Booking it upstairs, I sprinted out of the house like Val was hopping on a plane at that moment to come after me.

Thirty minutes later, I trudged through the front door. It was early enough that Jaxson was right where I left him—watching *Die Hard* in the living room. John McClane froze mid-shout.

"What's up? How'd it go?"

"I lost over one hundred and forty grand in ten minutes is how it went. How was your night?"

"How the fuck did you lose that kind of money?"

I flopped on the couch. "I'm not even sure myself. These guys— These guys are— They're Sams."

"Am I supposed to know what that means?"

"No," I said honestly. "I'm certain that no one is."

Chapter Five

*V*alentina

"Let me get this straight," I began. "You've been playing poker with public enemy number one behind my back—"

"I was letting you enjoy your vacation."

"You lost over one hundred grand—"

"When you think about it, I only lost ten grand. I didn't have the rest of the money long enough to get attached."

My eyes narrowed to slits. "And now you're in their gambling and fucking club."

"I think they... call them orgy clubs."

"Maverick!" Romeo stirred on my lap, awoken by the noise. The puppy crawled higher up and I cuddled him under my chin. "At least you behaved yourself while I was away."

"Actually, he peed in your shoe." Maverick climbed onto the bed and rested his head on the spot Romeo vacated. "I'm sorry," he said. "I should have told you."

"Yes, you should have." I smoothed a line over the ridges between his brows. "I wouldn't want you barreling toward me on the football field, but I have a feeling even you'd have trouble getting through six guys."

"They don't want to hurt me, Val. What they want is to pretend they're not like the average college guy chasing after booze and women. They're intellectuals too. Elite. This question game they play is another way to up the high of winning or losing everything, but this way they get to prove who is the smartest guy in the room. It's baboons showing off their butts."

"Why do they want you to be a part of it so badly?"

He shrugged. "I've got money and I can handle my own with them. Sawyer was also brimming about having an odd number. They've been looking for a seventh."

"How long would you guess they've been doing this? The gambling. The bets. The orgies."

"Don't know. Did you ever notice Aiden flashing more money than a guy with no job and middle-class parents should have?"

I tossed my head. "No. I've seen his car and it's pretty sweet. Otherwise the guy keeps it low-key. He doesn't flash gold watches or slide around in designer bomber jackets."

"He wouldn't. The bastard is too smart to draw attention like that."

A thought occurred to me. "Whatever these guys are about... do you think it's connected to the file he's keeping on the Sams? And while we're on the topic, were Nasir, Hayes, Rowen, and Winston in the file?"

Maverick's eyes flared. "No. Holy shit! No! Sawyer is but there's not one mention of those guys. Why in the fuck didn't I notice that before?"

"Because we're partners and this is what I'm here for." I flicked his forehead. "That's why you shouldn't do this without me."

His fingers curled through mine, bringing my palm to his lips. "The smartest person in the room... is always you, baby."

"Don't try to be sweet to me now," I replied, but the smile tugging at my lips gave me away.

Nala trotted out of the closet. She sniffed around, clearly searching for her baby. In a single bound she was on our bed, staring me straight in the eye for what was hers.

"Here you go, Mommy."

The dogs curled up on our pillow, making themselves right at home. I slipped away for two weeks and life continued on without me.

Ryder and I loved our time in Costa Rica, and as promised, we didn't do a lick of sightseeing. Feeding each other breakfast on the canopy. Bathing under a waterfall. Shedding the craziness of work and school and just being Valentina and Ryder for a brief pocket of time. It was—in a word—perfect.

Then we came home and stumbled on seven puppies that Adam was so attached to, he was guaranteed to bawl his eyes out when they had to return home to their owner. My baby's room was being gutted to remind me he wasn't a baby anymore. Jaxson picked up a bug and was home sick. Ezra picked up an assignment and was barely home at all. And, oh yeah, Maverick got in deep with a group of underground hedonists who are led by a guy who makes people disappear. Suddenly, I was reminded why I don't leave my boys on their own.

"Aiden and those four guys aren't in the file," I continued. "That's gotta mean something."

"We said the information could be used for blackmail. Well, what if the reason there isn't a record of what he's doing with the info is because he doesn't do anything with it? He collects it for the guys with the money, power, and knowledge of what having dirt like that on all of your future colleagues and opponents could do for you."

I nodded along. "Aiden is in the perfect position as president. He's in charge of all the guys and digging up secrets isn't a tradition he started, but it's one he can take full advantage of. We all have to share one devastating secret to get into the house, but Aiden's files have more than one. He has them all."

"As well as the ability to hide their tracks," Maverick said. "He buried their little black book so deep in his computer, I'm sure no one other than me could've found it."

"Wow," I breathed. "It's just a theory, but if it's true... Wow."

"Proving it has been our sticking point from the beginning. We can't get those guys on what the file *doesn't* say. Just because Aiden didn't collect information on them doesn't mean they're in on it."

"But we know there is a 'they' who is a part of this somehow and some way," I reminded. "I'll assume it's them until another batch of shady guys hanging around with Aiden and giving him seventy-thousand-dollar cars for no good reason, turns up." I inclined my head. "I'll also admit it can't stop with them. Sofia and I rounded up a lot of names we couldn't track down. This has been going on longer than your new friends have been around."

"It's like you said, Val. Tradition. They may not have started it, but they could be carrying on a scheme another Sally or Sam thought of. It's not like we haven't seen something like this before."

A chill skittered up my spine.

Maverick flipped onto his back. "But why Sawyer?" he asked, mostly to himself. "If those guys are behind this, why have Sawyer taken off the street? Where has he really been all of this time? And why, when he comes back, would he hook up with the men who kidnapped him? Unlike the rest of them, Sawyer is in that file. If there's a club, he joined it late."

"Maybe his and Teagan's silence about what truly happened is their admittance into the club."

"They lost over a year of their life. Would playing poker and fucking in a basement be worth that to you?"

"Definitely not. There has to be more to it than that. Money," I declared, "and probably a lot of it."

"I have to find out what's really going on here, Val. Whatever this is, it's not good."

"The sticking point for me is why it has to be you?"

"I'm in with them."

"They *let* you in," I corrected. "Invited you into their odd game out of nowhere. I'm supposed to believe Aiden doesn't have another motive? He has a hidden agenda behind going to the toilet. You're not a Sam, Maverick. Why would Aiden need a guy who is suspicious of him to be his seventh?"

"I can only find out by playing along."

I huffed, dropping my head back on the pillow. "Are you seeing how that's an extraordinarily bad idea? Please tell me you are."

Maverick took my hand and placed it on his chest. His heart pumped a steady rhythm beneath my fingers, seeking me through his rib cage. I couldn't tell you why that soothed me in every argument we had. All the same, it did.

"It's not by chance they're dragging me into this. The play is obvious. If they can get me on board, I—and therefore you—will drop it. The trick is to let them think their play is working."

"You're not doing this without me."

Nala barked, chiming in with her determination to not be left out either.

Maverick shut us both down. "Nope. I won't let you deeper into this than you already are."

"Come on, love. I'm your girlfriend. Aiden is assuming you're telling me every detail of what they get up to. He thinks I'm deep in this, so why shouldn't I be?"

"Val—"

"You told me they have their girlfriends, dates, and duchesses down there with them. Give me one good reason I can't be there too."

"Because excluding that one time Ezra and I double fingered you in the backseat—"

My face lit on fire at the memory.

"—group sex isn't my thing."

I swatted him with a pillow. "I wasn't suggesting we get naked with them. We'll dip out when they unroll the condoms."

"Maybe this isn't a good idea."

"Ooooh," I crowed. "Now that I'm on board, it's not a good idea?"

"We don't know how dangerous these guys are yet. Granted Teagan and Sawyer came back without a scratch. It still doesn't prove they're not above hurting people." He grasped my chin in a gentle grip. "And no one is hurting you."

"Of course not. Because you'll have my back and I'll have yours. This is the only way we do this, Maverick." I spoke over his oncoming refusal. "Say yes."

He argued some more. Insisted it wasn't safe and the best place for me was a thousand miles away from Aiden Connelly. I held firm.

"Okay," he finally said. "Yes."

Nala barked her acceptance.

"HOW WAS COSTA RICA?"

"It was magic. I'm serious. I'm pretty sure there were fairies flitting through the trees and sprites swimming under the waterfall. It was almost impossible to leave."

"Wow. Your boyfriend just whisked you away out of the blue?" Kendra sighed over her bowl of ground beef mush. "Where do I find these romantics? I'm serious. Was there a number you called? Or a website I should be signing up with?"

I chuckled. "Trust me, I got those guys the hard way. A website or phone call would've been much easier."

"Sawyer is romantic like that," Teagan mused. "He surprises me with flowers on the doorstep and trips to the beach because it's where we had our first kiss." A grin played on her lips. "Don't tell anyone—especially him—but I think he's working up the courage to propose."

Eve gasped. "Really? What will you say if he does?"

This is what my time with my stray sisters was all about. We got together, made yummy food, watched movies, and dished about everything that went on in our lives. I was shocked to admit how much I enjoyed it.

A big part of me wishes this could be every day with the Sallys. No pressure. No seventy-five minutes of clocked intense exercise or minimum grade point averages. No undercurrent of seriousness in everything we do—even bonding activities.

"How is it going in here, ladies?"

No Jade Ortega.

"Great," said Sabrina. "Val dug up a recipe for meatball-stuffed garlic bread. We're eating it in honor of our movie for tonight. *Inception* is a dream within a dream, so we're eating a food within a food."

"Clever. Anything I can help you with?"

Teagan looked around. "Kendra is on the meatballs. Eve and I are doing the sauces. Sabrina is rolling out the dough and Val's putting the final creation together. Are we allowed to ask you to make the cocktails? Manhattans?"

Jade peeked at the whiskey and vermouth on the kitchen counter. "I definitely didn't pick those up with this month's groceries. But you are all over twenty-one." She winked. "I don't see why not."

"All right." Teagan clicked her tongue. "You've just earned yourself a spot on the couch eating calorie-laden heart attacks of deliciousness and feasting on Leonardo DiCaprio."

"It's my lucky night." Charmed by Teagan, Jade joined our group. I didn't blame her. Teagan was the charming sort.

But is she the sort to trade her silence in exchange for Aiden and his friends' offer of... what?

I returned from Costa Rica a week and a half ago. Since then I settled into the same routine with the girls, and if Teagan noticed me watching her a little closer, she gave no sign of it.

There'd been another poker game the Friday that passed. Maverick up and decided not to go—likely owing to my promise to jump through the car window as he sped off, determined not to let him go there alone.

Unfortunately, he didn't have forever to fob them—and me—off. We had a month left of summer vacation and who knew if they'd continue their weekly games with a bunch of Sams overhead.

I should ask her about it. Like Aiden, she's gotta assume Maverick told me everything. I have always favored the direct approach.

"Teagan, can we talk after we're done?"

"Sure," she replied. She didn't sound the slightest bit worried about the conversation. "How much should we make?"

"Let's finish off the dough. If we can't eat it all, I'll bring it home to my boys."

"You're so mature and evolved, Val." Eve slid in next to me, carrying her bowl of marinara sauce. "One relationship can be tricky. You have four and you make it look so easy. How'd you convince them all to be okay with it?"

"Believe it or not, they didn't need convincing. I was the one twisting myself into knots about dating four guys and thinking I'd lose all of them if I suggested it. While the whole time they thought it was the obvious solution to being in love with the same girl."

Kendra groaned. "Okay, seriously, prez. Do not hold out on me with this number! Where do I find guys like this?!"

"Kendra, you are adorable stuffed in Mary Janes and wrapped in a winning bow of smart and witty. You don't need a number."

"Ah. You're so good for my self-esteem, Val."

I snorted. I truly liked this bunch. I would protect them from Aiden and whatever his true motives are. Even if his rich buddies Hayes, Nasir, Rowen, and Winston are involved. Even if Teagan is too.

The girls finished off the prep and passed their creations on to me. One by one, they trickled out of the kitchen, moving into the living room, until it was just me and Teagan. She picked up a slice of dough and a meatball, working side by side with me.

"You wanted to talk to me about something?"

"It's about the poker games."

"Ahh." She reached around me for the garlic sauce. "I wondered when you were going to ask me about that."

"I didn't really know what to ask. Maverick explained and I still don't get it. A couple of guys playing poker. Sure. Partying in the basement with your friends, girlfriends, and boyfriends. I understand that too. But the questions? Betting it all? Maverick losing over a hundred grand because tribalism benefits society? What's the point of all of that?"

"Honestly, I don't know who started the club or why. It was here long before any of us came to Somerset."

"The club?"

"They don't have a name. Or at least, I haven't heard the guys use it. All I know is they've been around since 2005."

A memory flitted out and floated to the surface. "2005? That's the same year the president of Nu Alpha Theta started the initiation."

Coincidence? I think not.

She shrugged. "Maybe. Zeta Rho and Nu Alpha are about pushing us to our limits. The club is about having *no* limits. They can get pretty intense, but they're harmless. In the end, it's just friends having fun, and everyone likes Maverick." She gave me a wry smile. "There isn't some grand conspiracy behind asking him to join. He isn't going to be *taken*."

Teagan laughed at her joke. I didn't.

"You can't say who started it, but there's a strong possibility—bordering on certainty—that it was a Sally or Sam. Aiden, Sawyer, and the rest of them are Sams. So yeah, I'd assume something is up when they suddenly ask a non-Sam to join."

"It's not in the rules that a non-Sally or Sam can't join. You know that."

I blinked. "I know that? Why would I know that?"

She expelled an impatient breath. "It was in the book. Didn't you read it?"

"The book?"

"Yes," she said slowly. "The book you got when you became president. It talked about the club and its rules. That's what Aiden said was in his book anyway."

"Teagan, I never got any book. I got an email forward from Jade explaining my duties, but no book."

"Really? But you were supposed to get it from—" Wincing, she stopped. "Oh. I'm sorry. Of course, you didn't get it. I'm such an idiot."

"Why?"

"Because you were supposed to get it from your predecessor... and she died."

Leighton.

"On top of that, Reagan left," she continued. "Without them here there was no one to pass it on to you."

What Leighton said to me all those months ago in her bedroom came roaring back.

"I won't talk to you or anyone. How I get my information is a presidential secret. If you want to know, you'll have to take over Zeta Rho Sigma."

"They pass it down from president to president," I whispered.

"Yep. You should ask Aiden to let you see his book. He didn't give us all the details, but he explained we're just continuing what others started."

"Messing around in a basement and discussing human nature is what they started?"

She smiled. "They do more than that."

"Care to elaborate?"

"Care to join us and find out for yourself?"

I stepped back, studying her. "I do," I said after a moment. "I'm more than willing to find out for myself, but I still want to know why you were too. Maverick says a lot of money is thrown around down there. Rich boys and their games don't hold back, but I would've thought you, Sawyer, and Aiden had more to lose."

"We do," she admitted. "Isn't that what makes it more fun? The only things worth having in life are the things you're afraid to lose. Family. Friends. Careers. Love. Sawyer was looking at a life mapped out for him by his father. He's only at Somerset because his dad pays his tuition, and he made it clear he was supporting one path and one path only. His.

"Sawyer didn't have choices until he joined the club. The night they initiated him, he earned ten grand. He wins some and he loses some," she continued, "but right now we're sitting on enough to have a future." Teagan stilled, hands frozen in the dough. "I watched my mom slowly lose a battle against her own body. Everything she worked for her whole life gone, and she couldn't lift a finger to stop it. After going through something like that, you realize what's truly important. And a little risk is worth going after it." She dropped her gaze. "You probably don't get that—"

"No." I squeezed her hand. "I understand risking everything for your future. I've put everything—even my life—on the line so that I could be where I am today." I dropped my voice, peering hard into her eyes. "But I didn't do it alone. If you're in trouble or in over your head, you can tell me, Teagan. I will do whatever I can to help you."

She scrunched up her face. "Why would I be in trouble? Because of the club?"

"Because I know there's more behind your disappearance than you're saying. You can deny it and pretend everything is fine, but I know it's not. Things have not been fine in this sorority for a very long time."

Her expression smoothed out, drawing blank.

"You can talk to me or not. Either way, I'll find out what's going on."

"There's nothing going on."

"But there is." I smiled.

"Ladies?" Jade cut through the tension. "Everything all right in here?"

I raised my voice. "Everything is fine, Jade. I'm putting the garlic bread meatballs in the oven now."

"Wonderful."

We stood there long after she was gone, locked in an unwavering gaze. Teagan was first to break.

"I won't confess to something that never happened, Val."

I lifted my shoulders. "You don't have to. Like I said, I'll find out either way."

"You do that." Teagan backed out of the room. "You know, life isn't one big conspiracy. Someone isn't always trying to pull something over on you."

"Yes, they are." I returned to my meatballs, calmly folding and laying them out. "If you don't think so, it means they've already fooled you."

MAVERICK

"I just got off the phone with Candace."

"What's the verdict?"

I tipped over the chip bag and littered a little salty goodness around Adam's sandwich. He was taking lunch out on the terrace like the lordly gentleman he'd become. But even lordly gentlemen liked peanut butter and banana sandwiches with a side of kettle chips.

My mother called me halfway through Dad duty to fill me in on the dog situation.

"Her plan was to breed Nala," she said. "Purebred blue heelers go for a thousand dollars a pop. Unfortunately, this particular litter—"

"—was sired by a roving tramp."

"Precisely. She won't be back for another month, but in the meantime, she's happy to hire a pet sitter to take them off your hands."

"She can consider me the pet sitter. Turns out, we like having them here. Milo and Teddy kept Jaxson company while he was sick. And

Olivia has claimed Dixie. I'm serious. She said she'll fight anyone who tries to take her."

Mom's laugh rang through the phone. "You can tell her that won't be necessary. Candace plans to find new homes for all of the puppies, so if you want one, she says you guys have first pick."

I stopped at the sliding glass door so Adam didn't overhear the conversation. "We definitely want one. Maybe two. Adam's been great with them. Very responsible. Val thinks he's ready for a pet."

"Your father is interested too. Because we don't have enough pets," she said under her breath.

"Mom, all you'd have to do is hold Chester and you'll melt like a popsicle."

"My track record with resisting you boys and your animals speaks for itself. I love you, darling. See you soon."

"Bye, Mom."

I went outside and set Adam's lunch in front of him. The chair beside him held a brown wicker basket and a little mewling Pepper who was trying to figure out how to escape. Adam had taken strongly to her. She was at the top of our list for his puppy surprise.

Plopping down on the other seat, I inhaled a deep breath. Today was the kind of perfect day that made even the most miserable shut-in want to be outside smelling the roses.

"We should go to the beach," I announced. "What do you think, little man?"

"Yeah," he cried. "Can Pepper come too?"

"Pepper's not quite ready for the beach. How about I round up the daddies and we'll meet Mom there?"

"Okay."

Two hours later, I was packing Adam and the beach gear in the car. Val called as I hopped in the front seat.

"I hear we're going to the beach," she said.

"Too good a day to waste it. You can join us or steal this opportunity to have alone time. Steam in the tub with a book and your chocolate stash."

"Tempting. Very tempting. But I can do that tonight after we put Adam to bed. I'd rather be with my boys."

"We'll be at the beach house. You have a suit and everything there, right?"

"I do, but it's an old one. Doesn't fit right now that the Sallys have me packing on the muscles. Mind grabbing me one from our room?"

"Of course."

I hung up, twisted to tell Adam I'd be right back, and hurried upstairs. Jaxson, Ezra, and Ryder went on ahead to open the house and check to make sure we were stocked up in case we spent the night. Olivia and Caroline were staying in. Caroline invited a few friends over for dinner, and she and Olivia intended to enjoy an evening with members of their generation.

I bounded up the stairs and spun at the top for my room. My cell buzzed in my hand.

"Hey, babe," I greeted. "Need something else?"

"I could do without you calling me babe." A dry, distinctive voice filled my ear. "Bad time, Rick?"

"No." I slowed to a stop. "What do you want, Aiden?"

"You missed the game last week. I'm wondering if you're no longer interested in hanging out."

"My girlfriend came back from vacation. I was interested in spending time with her. I'm still on for the game if you guys are."

"We are," he stated. "This Saturday. Nine o'clock. I'm sure she's not waiting for an invitation, but tell Valentina I can't wait to see her there."

"You understand we're there for the game and *only* the game."

"Whatever you want. It's up to you how many of the after-game activities you partake in."

"How many other activities are there to partake in?" I asked.

"You'll see."

Click.

I swore under my breath. I knew I'd have to go back and I knew Valentina was resolved to go with me. I just didn't think I'd have less than three days to talk her out of it.

"NOT HAPPENING."

Val pressed the chocolate-covered strawberry to my lips.

The two of us lounged on a beach towel. Legs tangled. A bowl of treats between us. A perfect day lending us more fortune with a light, cool breeze and a nearly empty beach. Jaxson, Adam, and the guys raced through the surf. Their shouts mingled with the crashing waves and invited us to join. Everything was set up for a flawless family outing.

If not for Aiden Connelly.

"Val—"

She shoved the strawberry in, laughing as I coughed around it. Val took the chance to get ahead of my argument.

"I spoke to Teagan today," she began. "She told me the club has been around for years and I would've known that already if I had been given the book."

"Book?" I asked around my mouthful.

"A book passed down from president to president. In it there's supposedly an explanation of the club and its rules. The way she made it sound, I get the feeling the club is like the frat on steroids. She didn't give me enough details for me to be sure, but she did say it was never limited to frat brothers or sorority sisters."

"We need to see that book."

She grinned. "I thought you'd say that." Closing the scant distance between us, Val nipped my chocolatey lips. I was on her in a blink, pushing her giggling into the sand, and deepening the kiss. Sweet cacao, sun, wind, and Val swirled in an intoxicating mix, scattering my neat, organized mind into disarray.

Our tongues and moans entwined. I fisted sand to keep my hands from roaming her body. If I touched her, that bathing suit was coming off.

My cock twitched at the mere thought of making love to Val on the beach.

She giggled, feeling the shameless thing begging against her thigh. "Down, boy. Our son is ten feet away."

"Our bedroom is two yards away." My voice was a low gruff. "I'll race you there."

"And I'll give you a head start if"—she trailed her finger over my lips—"you promise we're in this together."

I came down like she threw a bucket of seawater in my face. "That's cheating."

"I know, right?" Her impish smirk enticed me not to care. "I've got a few more sexual tricks up my sleeve to get you on board. You can pretend I haven't already and let me run through the whole seduction."

"I will take that option. Let a man preserve some of his dignity."

Her throat bobbed as she laughed. I couldn't resist kissing the soft, unblemished skin.

"Think Aiden will give you the book?"

"Now that I know about it, what would his excuse be for not letting me see it? I'm president now. Refusing would make him look shadier than he already is." Val draped her arms around my shoulder, drawing me in to rest in the crook of her neck. "I've been a Sally for two years and their president for one. I can't believe I didn't get a whiff that this club existed. I wonder who started it and why."

"Tribalism," I said softly. "That instinctual urge to create an us versus them even within the most exclusive groups. The Sallys and Sams won't be the first to create a secret collegiate society. Yale had Skull and

Bones. The University of Virginia has the Seven Society. Rutgers has several."

"The book must outline what the criteria are. I bet Aiden handpicks the guys he wants like he picked you. If he went around shouting about it in the Sam house, I would've known earlier. Why do you think he wants you?"

I shook my head, brushing my nose along her throat. "I don't think he did. Sawyer invited me to the game. The whole time I was there, I felt like I was auditioning. Sawyer wanted me in and the guys approved."

"Are we thinking that this club is behind everything? The disappearances. Aiden's file."

"I think we're finally closer to figuring out the truth."

She heaved a sigh. "In that case, I better get you upstairs and make my case for why I should join the club too." Val tilted my head up. "I'm sure you'll find my arguments very persuasive."

I lurched to my feat, hoisting a shrieking Val in the air. Apparently that Aiden shit couldn't ruin everything.

Chapter Six

Valentina

"Val, are you sure about this? An undercover spy, you are not."

"What's that supposed to mean?" I held a pair of Tiffany diamond butterflies to my ears, thought better of it, and reach for the hoops instead. "I'm stealthy."

Sofia snorted from her comfortable spot on Maverick's chaise. She had no less than five puppies on her lap and was loving every minute of them. "You are filter-less, my friend. Don't think I didn't overhear the throwdowns between you and Aiden in the council meetings. He, or anyone there, will say something that pisses you off and you'll let them have it right in the ass."

"Ugh. Don't give me that visual." Earrings chosen, I stepped into the closet to pick my shoes. "I'll be on my best behavior tonight," I called out to her. "If their guards are down, they'll tell me everything I need to know about this club."

"It won't be that easy, Val. It never is. Didn't Teagan mention an initiation?"

"She did. How bad would you guess it is?"

"I know a couple of guys that had to shave their heads. These secret societies don't mess around, boo."

My Caverley ankle boots winked at me from the other side of the closet. They'd been spared Romeo's outside-the-pee-pad accidents and begged for a night out before they became the next target.

"Unless they ask me to do something illegal, I'll stick it out." I pulled on my boots and stepped out, twirling for Sofia. "How do I look?"

"I'd definitely hop on your ass when the orgy starts."

"Shut up." I nabbed a pillow and lobbed it at her head.

"Hey!" She laughed. "You can't throw things at me when I'm holding puppies."

"That's not a rule." Although a peek in the mirror confirmed I was on the right side of gorgeous.

My black lace dress flirted just above my knee, but the front slit cut higher still. The dress itself was effortlessly beautiful in its simplicity. My finishing touches—diamond choker, classy earrings, and boots—put the entire ensemble over the edge.

"Do you need to get this dressed up to hang out in the Sams' basement?"

"Maverick says the dress code ranges from Vera Wangs to sneakers and puka shells. I'm falling somewhere in between."

"Val, seriously. Do you want me to go with you? We'd be outnumbered but between the three of us, we'll put up a hell of a fight."

I bunched in next to her, hugging her tight. "Thank you, but we'll be okay. Besides, your godson is looking forward to baking cakes with you."

"I can't leave my date hanging," she murmured. "Are you sure you'll be okay?"

"I'm sure. I'll text you every hour if that'll make you feel better."

"It will."

A knock preceded Maverick entering our bedroom. "Ready to go?"

He opted for somewhere in the middle too. In Maverick's case, him on the laid-back spectrum was Boris Kodjoe. The "suit, cuff links, and gold tie pin" spectrum was Tyson Beckford. The man looked like a supermodel in everything he wore and the blue blazer and black jeans did nothing to tone him down.

If there is an orgy, they'd be hopping on his ass first. Damn. Maybe Sofia's right about needing backup.

"Maverick, did you get a chance to talk to the owner?" Sofia asked.

"Shit, yeah, I did. They're giving them all away, so if you want one, claim them."

Sofia squealed. Picking up one of the dogs, she kissed all over his yapping head. "I'll take Blue."

"And I'll take you." Maverick held out a hand for me. "Unless you've changed your mind and decided to bake cakes with your best friend and favorite son."

"I did not." I grasped him firmly. "Night, Sof. I'll text you later."

Maverick and I left the house with no further arguments or plys for me to stay.

We arrived at the Sam house at nine o'clock on the dot. Aiden came out as Maverick held open my door.

"Good. You're here. We can leave."

"Leave?" Maverick repeated. "Why would we leave?"

"We switch up locations of the game, so people don't ask what we're doing in the basement every week," he explained like it was obvious. "Let's go. We're taking my car."

"No. We'll follow behind you."

"No. You won't. Nasir's guards only let in guests who have their license numbers on the approved list. His parents' rule, not Nasir's. They won't let you pass the gates unless you're riding with me."

Jaw tight, Maverick shared a look with me. He didn't want me there at all. Discovering we were being taken to an undisclosed location and wouldn't be able to leave on our own might be the nail in the coffin that made him stick me in the car and go home.

"Hurry up. I'm parked in lot 4G." Aiden strolled down the walkway and turned up the street. He didn't consider waiting for us.

"Forget this, Val," Maverick hissed. "We're going home."

My love is as wonderful as he is predictable.

"He's taking us to his friend's house, not an underpass cockfight." I rubbed his shoulders. "Relax. Everything's fine. And if for one second it's not, we'll call Ezra to come get us. Okay?"

"He could've told us we were going somewhere else. Better yet. We could've met him outside of the gates. He's messing with us and I'm not about it."

"Aiden Connelly would jerk his nana around for shits and giggles. It's second nature to him by this point. Don't let him distract us from what we're here to do."

"Are you guys coming?!"

Maverick kissed me. A soft brush of the lips.

"I know, baby," I whispered.

We didn't say anymore.

Silently, we gathered our things from the car and followed Aiden to the parking garage. He led us up to the top floor where a lone Jaguar gleamed under the flickering fluorescents.

I wonder how he'll explain his newest possession to his parents. Of course that assumes he truly was born, and not stitched together by an absentminded mad scientist who forgot his heart.

"Want to ride up front, Val?" he asked.

"Thanks, I'm good."

He shrugged a telltale *suit yourself.*

"What's the address?" Maverick demanded.

"Why? Going to give it to friends so they'll storm the place if you're a minute past midnight?" He tsked though Maverick didn't confirm it. "You gotta trust a little, Rick."

The ride to Nasir's was as awkward as the silence smothering us. Aiden drove us in the opposite direction of where we came, taking us further from Evergreen Estates. It was only when he turned on Seabreeze that I realized where we must be going.

"The beach?"

Aiden nodded.

"Nasir's a commuter, isn't he?" A handsome face and three-pierced ear floated in my mind. "Winston too."

"And Rowen and Hayes," he confirmed. "They don't spend a lot of time in the Sam house except for bonding activities. And the parties."

"I vaguely recall those guys. But I don't see why a bunch of guys too busy to hang around would be chosen for your club out of everyone."

"Your guess is as good as mine," he said easily. "They were chosen by my predecessor. I inherited them. Cool bunch of guys, though."

"Why—"

"That's the house on the end." Aiden pointed through the window. "5637 Seabreeze Lane. Feel free to text your security detail."

Maverick said nothing. My man didn't respond to bait.

I turned to the window as our beach house flashed by. Hard to imagine it was a few days ago that I collected shells with Adam, learned to make seared scallops with Ryder, kissed Maverick on the sand, and basked in the sunset on a perfect day with my family.

I watched the house until it disappeared behind half a dozen more. "Name?"

A flashlight sought me through the window, beaming directly into my corneas.

"Aiden Connelly, Maverick Beaumont, and Valentina Moon," said Aiden.

A stout, hefty man bent and put his head half into the car. "My information says this car is registered to Winston Abernathy."

"Winston lent me his car indefinitely."

The guy pulled out and went into his booth. A few minutes passed and I assumed he was calling back up to help chase us away. The thought no sooner crossed my mind than the gates rumbled open.

Nasir Harb's beachside paradise was built in the same style as many houses on this lane—ours included. Windows upon windows made up the grand house and allowed me a peek into nearly every room.

A butler met us in the driveway, opening our door and bowing us inside. "The master and his guests are in the second living room."

"I know the way, Klein," Aiden said. "Thanks."

Years of living and loving my boys made me no stranger to the finer things. I was used to wealthy homes filled with astonishingly expensive knickknacks that served no function other than looking pretty. Which is why Nasir's home threw me.

The cream-painted walls didn't boast dozens of paintings from artists I never heard of. An antique hutch full of plates no one was allowed to eat off of didn't greet me in the entryway. By wealthy people's standards, Nasir's home of family photos, scattered leather couches, and mahogany shelves bordered on... ordinary.

But ordinary people don't live in forty-five-million-dollar homes.

We walked into the living room and nine pairs of eyes landed on us.

And they don't host secret society parties in Mommy's second family room.

"Rick." A man in a purple shirt and white pants waved to my boyfriend. His ascot told me he was Winston without me having to recall his name. Standing next to him was a petite blonde wearing the very Tiffany earrings I decided against. She was the only girl I didn't recognize by sight.

"Sabrina? Kendra? Eve?" I gaped at my sisters.

The three of them took up the ottoman with Teagan. At least they had the decency to look sheepish.

Weeks of hanging out, watching movies, and going for runs, they forgot to drop this tidbit into the conversation.

"Val, you know everyone," said Aiden.

Is it me or is that ass smirking?

"Except for the duchess, Phillipa."

Winston's companion came over to shake my hand.

"I set up the table upstairs," Nasir said, "but there's no rush. Chill. Eat. Drink."

The guys here I knew in passing. I recognized them from Sally-Sam parties, and as Hayes handed Eve a drink, a memory of the two of them making out against the kitchen counter resurfaced. Eve called her boyfriend Ben.

Hayes Benson.

Why does it feel like during my normal summer of fun, I was being played for a fool the entire time?

"Val, come sit with us."

I slipped out of Maverick's hold, striding up to them on their ottoman. Kendra tugged me down.

"I can tell exactly what you're thinking and we're sorry," she rushed out. "We wanted to tell you, but you can't talk about the club with people who aren't in it. Please don't hate us."

"Did you guys really stay on campus for school?" I returned. "Or was it for the club?"

"School, of course," said Sabrina. "We haven't spent the last several weeks lying to your face. We wouldn't do that. We just kept our private business private."

I scoffed. "I'd believe that if I wasn't president. Why would a secret society for Sams and Sallys be a secret from me?"

"When you didn't start the club for the Sallys, we figured it was a part of your 'leave the silly traditions in the past' promise," Eve spoke up. "We assumed you wanted to be left out of it, so we did."

"Who is we? How many of you are there?"

"Just us and Heather and Crista," Teagan said. "We were chosen by Leighton."

The same Leighton who pretended you didn't exist the first time I asked her about you.

"New Sallys can't join unless you, the new president, choose them."

I shook my head, gaze sweeping the mingling coeds. "That won't be happening until I know exactly what this is about."

"Aiden's over there." Teagan pointed at the tinted windows. "Ask him."

I was up and off, ending the conversation. My feelings over the girls keeping this from me was a mess I'd untangle later. Right then, Aiden and I were long overdue for a chat.

Sea air wrapped around me as I pushed onto the balcony. The playful wind teased my hair, swaying the hem of my dress, and imparting a light chill though it was a warm night.

"Aiden."

"Valentina."

My counterpart leaned on the railing, looking out over the sea. I joined him.

"Ever feel like you're still a guest in this world." Soft words floated to my ear, fighting the wind that threatened to snatch it away. "You have the house, the cars, the family, and a future that promises it won't disappear. And yet, your past will always keep you on the outside."

"Yes." The reply spilled from my lips unbidden. "I know that feeling."

"They say the world is a different place outside of college. I say college is the audition and life is the show. We're nervous, panicked, and holding on to a thread of hope that we'll be good enough to make it. Then we're thrown onstage to have every move, line, and action scripted for us. We've spent all this time preparing to be the lead character in someone else's story. Never truly free."

"It can feel like that sometimes, but that stage doesn't have to be our reality."

"Why?"

"Because even the most faithful actor knows when to improvise."

He chuckled. "You may be right."

We fell into a silence that was, dare I say it, companionable.

"I want to see that book, Aiden."

Obviously, I ruined it.

"I assumed so." Aiden reached into his pocket and held something up between us. A small, black book clutched between two fingers.

"You carry it around with you?"

"I knew you'd ask to see it when Teagan told me you talked."

"Why didn't you tell me about it yourself? The book? The club? Why, Aiden?"

He shrugged. "You didn't ask."

"I didn't ask? Are you serious? You know very well that I didn't know to ask. You— You're a sun-baked asshole!"

Okay. Sofia might have a point about me being filter-less.

He burst out laughing. "What the hell does that mean?"

"You know what it means." I snatched the book from his hand. "But I take it back anyway. You're actually a spit-roasted asshole with douchebag on top and a side of arrogant fucker."

"All right, all right." I thought he might tip off the balcony guffawing. "I should have told you. I admit. I'm going to really blow your mind and say... I'm sorry." Aiden stuck out his hand. "Truce?"

I eyed the appendage. "Depends. Are you or this book going to explain why you had Sawyer taken away?"

"I didn't."

"Then you can put that back where it was."

Aiden let out a breath like I was the most irritating person on this balcony. "Just read it. Then you'll understand."

"What will I understand, Aiden? What's in this book that you can't tell me yourself? Like you should have done a year ago."

He swept out his hand. "You want to know what the club's about? It's simple. We stretch ourselves to the limit. No holding back or hesitation. The Sams and Sallys acquire the best Somerset has to offer and the club finds out how far they'll go."

"And you do that by losing money, tossing questions at each other, and having sex in a basement?"

"We do that by shedding all constraints. When is the last time you had a deep, intellectual conversation with someone you weren't dating? Years? Never?"

"I haven't really thought about it."

"Of course." A fervency laced his tone. "Because it's not in our script. We're supposed to make polite, meaningless small talk with everyone we meet and never say anything real. What we do is strip away the bullshit and take what we want."

"So... it's a club for hedonists?"

"No, Valentina. It's so much more."

I glanced back at the room full of people. "What do you all get from this? The thrill of secrecy? Money? A boys and girls club that you can seek favors from for the rest of your life?"

"None of the above. What we want is improvisation."

I nodded slowly, tracing the design etched in the book's leather. "Why did you choose Maverick?"

"It was getting tricky with an even number. Too many ties. I wanted a guy that wouldn't piss himself being in a room with Winston and the rest of them. Plus, Sawyer could vouch for him. He's smart. Doesn't take any shit. And any twenty-one-year-old guy already tied down with a kid, pets, mortgage, and pseudo-wife would be looking to blow off some steam."

"Fuck you." I meant that with every fiber of my soul. "Maverick doesn't feel tied down."

"He wouldn't tell you if he did."

I erased the distance between us, getting in his face. "That's cute. You hang out with him a handful of times and convinced yourself you know him better than I do. Maverick loves his life. He has friends that support him. A son that looks up to him. His dream job on the other end of graduation. And a pseudo-wife that gives one hell of a blow job." I smiled sweetly. "He's not looking for cheap thrills."

Aiden bore my speech—nodding along with his lips pushed out. "Then why"—he leaned in until our noses brushed—"does he keep coming back to us?"

Because he's going to find out what the fuck you're really about, Aiden Connelly.

My jaw clenched tight, keeping that thought inside. Too late. It should've held back the rest of what I said too. Acting like we had no reason to be here would give Aiden license not to invite us back.

"Because he enjoys a good game of poker," I finally said. "Also, I think you have him intrigued with your question game. Why throw that in?" I waved the book between us. "Is it one of the rules?"

"It's a rule that members have to stretch themselves in every way. That includes intellectually. I told Maverick this the other night. You should stand by your beliefs so strongly, you'd hang everything on them. Anything less is bullshit."

"Why—"

The door creaked open. Maverick encompassed the entrance, taking in the scant distance between us. "Everything okay, Val?"

"Everything's fine. Aiden gifted me with some light reading. I know what I'll be doing tonight."

"Wait till you get to chapter three," Aiden said. "It's a page-turner." He pushed off the rail, loping for the other door, and letting himself inside. "Game starts in ten, Rick."

Maverick closed it behind him. "Sure you're okay?"

"I am. Why?"

He gathered me in his arms, resting my head on his chest, and rubbed soothing hands on my back. "You were making your I'm-inches-away-from-throwing-you-off-this-balcony face."

"That's my normal face around Aiden. He threw some garbage at me, saying he kept me in the dark because I didn't ask. Not to mention Kendra, Eve, Teagan, and Sabrina pulling the same excuse. I became president to find out what's going on in my house and put a stop to it." I snaked my arms around his waist, holding him tight. "So naïve. Everyone's keeping secrets, Maverick. I never knew where to begin."

"Do you want to blow this off? Forget Aiden. I'll call us a car and we'll be home in thirty minutes with people who aren't so duplicitous that we question their real motive when they claim they have to leave to take a shit."

A laugh burst out of me. "I'd love to choose option A. But we came here for a reason, and if this book doesn't tell me what I want to know, Aiden will give me the rest." I kissed the skin peeking from his shirt. "Instead, distract me with sweet things for the next five minutes, and then let's go inside and play duplicitous shit with the best of them."

"Hmm. Adam's going to love his new puppy." He chuckled. "The kid has us wrapped. He knew we'd give in and let him keep one. Or three."

"He is scarily hard to say no to, and Pepper's big brown eyes don't help."

"I'm going to my parents' house tomorrow. Dad wants a picture of the pups to scope out their newest addition. Mom wants another swing at convincing me to move home."

I shook my head, smiling. "I love Selah for how much she loves you. Twenty-one years old and you're still her baby boy."

"It's Mariana and Alison's fault. They didn't leave home until they were twenty-three and twenty-five."

Mariana and Alison were Maverick's older sisters. Both of them intelligent, funny, independent women who took me out for girls' night whenever they were in town. And both enjoyed their high-class luxury life in Evergreen Estates until marriage, kids, and new jobs took them away. They were in no kind of rush to leave home and Selah didn't complain.

"My mom wasn't properly prepared for her *baby* to leave the nest at eighteen. On top of that, she still sees my living at Ryder's house like one long extended sleepover. Back to when we were kids."

The slow, gentle circles on my back seeped tension from my bones. Waves crashed against the shore, singing a persistent lullaby that drew my eyes shut.

I loved this place. Cherished the memories I created here.

Making love with Jaxson for the first time.

Capturing the moment Adam saw his first jellyfish on camera.

Burying Ryder in the sand.

Kissing Maverick under the stars.

We weren't having an extended sleepover. We were a family.

"I see why she'd think that," I said. "Doesn't really feel like you've left when you're a few streets over. I've thought about what it'd be like to get our own place after college."

"Is that something you want?"

"If life takes us somewhere else, then I'd go happily. But somewhere along the way a miracle happened and I fell in love with Evergreen. Late-night talks with Caroline on the porch. Watching Adam run around the yard with his friends. Getting frisky with you in the promenade parking lot."

"That was two times."

"It might take time for your family to adjust," I continued, giggling. "But I feel we've found our place. Our home."

"I—"

"Yo, Rick." Rowen barreled onto the balcony. "You coming?"

"Yes. Give me a second."

Rowen ducked inside, leaving us alone.

"I feel the same," Maverick finished. "I'm where I'm supposed to be."

He bent his neck to take in the second floor. The windows let us see everything—including the guys finding their spot around a poker table.

Our five minutes were over. "I'll go up. You start reading that thing. Find out if there's a section on keeping encrypted files of data on your brothers."

"It's probably in chapter three," I mocked.

We shared one lingering kiss and then broke apart inside. Maverick headed upstairs and I wandered over to the impressive collection of drinks. Skipping the alcohol, I poured myself a glass of cranberry juice.

The girls gathered in front of the sound system, looking through the music selection. Teagan broke away and began pushing the furniture off the rug. They were gearing up for a dance party and I was gearing up to leave. My sisters and I had a lot to talk about, but I wanted peace and quiet with this book first.

I slipped out as Julien Kelland crooned through the speakers. The butler directed us to the second living room, which meant there was a first.

I returned the way we came and swung left at the end of the hallway. I ended up in a dining room. Continuing through the door at the end, I found what I was looking for. This living room was double the size of the other. The television hanging over the mantle rivaled most movie theater screens. All I needed was a chaise and a lamp.

I spotted both near the fireplace and got comfortable. The book cracked as I opened it—the binding lifting away from the spine. It had years on it and the evidence of changing hands. Owners who dog-eared the pages. Owners who read while eating lunch. Owners who scribbled in the margins.

I was supposed to believe this guide was passed from Sam president to Sam president. Also that somewhere there was one for me.

Flipping to page one, I started reading.

MAVERICK

"I've got a fresh deck." Winston tossed an unopened pack of cards on the table. "Just in case."

"Just in case what?" Nasir tossed back. "I marked them with invisible ink? Waiting for me to whip out my special sunglasses? You watch too many of those European caper movies."

"No, *you* watch too many of them. Can't have you getting ideas, mate."

Nasir chuckled, taking the accusation in stride. "Give it here."

Sawyer leaned over in his seat. "You got Val on board." His breath washed over me and with it the stench of Laphroaig scotch. "Does this mean you want in?"

"Thought I was in."

He laughed like I was joking. "Come on. It's not as easy as taking our money every week. You have to prove yourself and that you can run with the Sams." Gripping my shoulder, he shook me. "I don't doubt you will. You're not a Sam, but you should've been."

I was stuck on the "prove myself" part of the conversation. "What does that mean? What do you expect me to do?"

"Don't worry about it. You'll pass."

"Pass what?"

"Gentlemen," Hayes spoke. "Ready?"

Sawyer pulled back. Conversation over. "Let's do this."

VALENTINA

I closed the book an hour after sitting down.

Small book, short read, head chock-full of conflicting thoughts.

I headed back to the living room where the ladies were deep in their party. Half the bottles from the bar littered on and around the coffee table. They danced barefoot on the rug—jumping and whipping their heads like all they knew about dancing was flinging every limb around at once.

Teagan stayed out of the fray. I plopped beside her on the ottoman. My possible friend grabbed my feet and placed them on her lap.

"You ran away from us. All this too much for you?"

"I can handle a little dancing. I snuck away to do some reading."

She formed a small "o" with her mouth. "Aiden gave you the book. So, you get it now. Will we have a club for the Sallys?"

I shook my head. "I don't see that happening while I'm president. I have enough on my plate juggling school, Zeta Rho, and life at home. I can't take on half of what that book describes."

"That's fair. I forget you have a whole life outside of us." She swept the room. "I guess this all seems silly to you."

"No," I replied honestly. "No sillier than sororities, fraternities, anime clubs, film clubs, and all the other groups we form to find people interested in the same things as us. This particular Sam/Sally tradition is a bit hardcore, but that's not surprising either. When we do things, we go hard."

Teagan blew out a breath. "I'm so glad you understand. We all felt weird about keeping this from you."

"It wasn't on you to tell me. It was on Aiden, and you can believe I let his ass know what I thought about his silence."

"Aiden is... Aiden." Teagan tossed me a look and we laughed. For the first time ever, we were on the same page. "The guy is impossible to figure out."

"From your lips to the heavens," I said. "I've spent so much time around him and still feel like I know nothing about him."

"Val!"

I cried out as hands seized me.

"You're done being boring," Sabrina said. "Dance with us."

That seemed a reasonable request. Plus, no one craved dancing more than me. I let them drag me into the middle of their makeshift dance floor and threw myself into the music. Kendra sidled up to dance with me, whipping her head in a move I was dubbing the *electrocuted dance.* I had no idea why, but I ended up copying. We cracked up as the other girls joined us, hair swinging this way and that.

"Damn. I thought I'd walk in on something much sexier." A dry British sotto broke into our fun. In response, the duchess pounced and threw him on the couch. By where their hands were roaming, he would get sexy much quicker than he thought.

The boys shuffled into the room. Rowen and Hayes picked off my dance partners, claiming them for themselves. Sawyer and Aiden veered toward the drinks while Nasir collapsed on a couch free of Brits. One person was missing.

Nasir raised a brow when I sat down. "Uh. Rick made it clear he'd break every bone in our hands if we even thought about touching you, so—"

"Maverick's the nice one," I snapped, "because I'd break everything else."

He threw his hands up, chuckling. "I'm not thinking about it. I swear."

"Where is he?"

Nasir jerked his chin up. "Bathroom."

"Which one?"

"Upstairs. Third on the left."

I left him to his G-rated thoughts. The game was finally over, and we needed to talk.

Skirting Eve and Hayes, I made for the hallway.

"—fuck are you doing?"

A hiss pulled me up short.

Aiden and Sawyer stood behind the wet bar. Aiden's back was to me and his height blocked Sawyer's view. Neither one noticed me standing there.

"You're not doing this again, Sawyer. If you can't handle it, your ass goes home now."

"I c-can handle it." The small, wavering voice was night and day from the affably charming one that normally fell from his lips. "I'm sorry, Aiden."

"You better—"

Sawyer stepped to the side at that moment and spotted me. "Oh, hey, Val."

Aiden spun. I caught a flash of something disappear behind his back—too fast for me to make it out.

"Everything okay?" Sawyer tried for a smile that trembled around the edges. "Need a drink?"

"No, I was... just looking for Maverick." I took a step toward him. "Are you okay?"

He shrugged. "Fine."

"Sawyer, what are you doing over there?" Teagan called. "Come dance with me."

The smile smoothed out, lighting the eyes of the Sawyer I knew well. "My lady calls."

He pushed past us. I didn't watch him go. I remained fixed on Aiden.

My counterpart crooked a brow. "Something to say, Moon?"

"What's behind your back?"

"Nothing."

"You're lying."

His jaw ticced. For the first time, true irritation burned in his orbs. "I'll be honest, I'm getting real fucking sick of you treating me like the enemy."

I faced him, squaring up. "Want to show me I'm wrong? Turn around."

"There's nothing behind my back."

"Then there's no reason for you not to *turn around*."

"Fine." Aiden spun and concealed behind his back was—

—nothing.

I stepped closer but it made no difference. There was no obvious bulge in his pocket, his hands were empty, and the counter boasted nothing but alcohol.

"Is this the part where I get an apology?" he demanded.

My jaw clenched. Aiden was a particular kind of asshole. I stumble on him getting in Sawyer's face and he acts like he's the one who was wronged. But... it was another sort of asshole who didn't own up when they made a mistake.

"Sorry." The word burned coming out. "What's up with Sawyer?"

"Ask him yourself."

Aiden blew past me.

I resisted the urge to take back that apology or heed his taunt. Sawyer looked fine now as he danced with his girlfriend. I still needed to find Maverick before Aiden took back his book.

We crossed paths at the top of the stairs.

"Val—"

I grabbed his hand, tugging him toward the first door I laid eyes on. A peek inside confirmed it was a bedroom.

"Get in," I whispered for no reason. The music was too loud for them to hear me throw a vase. "The book. You have to see it."

"What's in it?"

I shut and locked us in. Maverick sat on the bed and then placed me on his lap. I handed over the book for him to read but launched into the whole thing anyway.

"It explains everything that Aiden said. They're brothers who are brothers in everything. Supporting each other without question. Willing to go as far as it takes to prove themselves. Under those terms, the president can pick anyone they believe fits the criteria. Doesn't have to be a Sally or Sam."

"Does it say anything about compiling files on everyone who walks into the house?"

I shook my head. "Nothing like that, but it does"—I flipped to page forty—"talk about this."

"Initiation," he read across the top. "To get into the club?"

"No. To get into the Sallys and Sams. Read it. Second paragraph."

He squinted at the cramped, handwritten text. "*The final test is the reveal of secrets. Sams must trust their brothers absolutely, and trust is only possible when you have nothing left to protect. Nothing left to hide. Those who refuse to reveal their secret will be denied a place in Nu Alpha Theta, but with the respect of their privacy being protected. To use, allude to, or reveal these secrets will mark you as without honor and unfit to lead Nu Alpha Theta.*"

"Holy hell," he breathed. "This reads like it was written by the High King of Evergreen to be bestowed upon his heir. Without honor? Unfit to lead? Who talks like that about running a fraternity?"

"You haven't gotten to the best part yet." I read it myself. "*When you've chosen the final candidates, contact this email address: ehqw873@appamail.com. You will receive a reply containing all the information you need for the initiation. Do not share with anyone.*"

Maverick leaned back, eyes wide. "This is it? You just shoot off a message to this email address and they tell you if the brother of one of your pledges is hiding from a gang?"

"It's unbelievable. Leighton said I had to become president to find out and here it is. The email of the person who told Leighton I killed someone."

Maverick shot up, tipping me onto the comforter. "Val, you have to contact this person. Find out who they are and how they know the things they do."

"That was my first thought, but why would they tell me? However they do it can't be legal. They're not going to shout about it—least of all to me. If they're connected to the Sallys, they know we don't have pledges and therefore no reason to contact them."

He started pacing, treading the length of the cashmere carpet. "You'll get pledges, Val. When school starts. When the time comes, they'll have to respond. In the meantime, I'll trace the address and see what comes up." He spun on me. "What else does the book say? Are we so lucky that we got the email address for body cleanup?"

"No. We're also missing the chapter on faking your death." Sighing, I tossed it on the bed. "It mostly goes on about what it takes to be a Sam and your duties to your brothers."

"That's fine, babe. It's already told us what we need to know." He knelt and rested his head on my lap. "We will figure this out. I promise."

"I know we will. And whoever is behind this, whether it's Leighton, Aiden, the club, or every Sally in the house—they're gonna fucking know it too."

Chapter Seven

M*averick*

"Daddy!"

A cannonball struck my chest, ejecting me from sleep. I shot up and knocked the giggling menace onto the covers.

"Daddy," Adam cried. "We have to walk Pepper before school."

"Y-yes," I rasped. "We will, son. Just give Daddy... five more minutes." I collapsed on my pillow, eyes drooping in an instant.

Soft lips brushed my forehead in a much sweeter wake-up call. "Sorry, love. You can't have five minutes. You slept through the alarm and your class starts at eight. Walk Pepper with Adam and I'll have breakfast sent up here."

My voice croaked from deep in my chest. "Sometimes being late is the only sane thing to do."

Val laughed. "Don't pass that on to our kid. It's hard enough getting him ready in the morning."

"Babe, please." I was reduced to begging. "If you give me five more minutes, I'll love you for all eternity."

"You'll do that anyway," she replied, amused.

Damn if she isn't right.

"But five minutes is yours. Come on, Adam. Let's see what's for breakfast. Pepper, you too, girl."

An enthusiastic yap was her response. After some shuffling, chatter, and barking, my room plunged into silence.

Summer was over and everyone in our home under the age of twenty-two was off to school. All except for Jaxson and, no, I didn't forget

132

Pepper. She was off to obedience school right after Val dropped Adam for his first day of elementary school.

What the hell possessed me to sign up for an eight a.m. class?

Val's seminar in health psychology starts at eight, a voice reminded me. *You came in your pants dreaming about riding to school together.*

There was one thing for certain in this big, crazy world of ours.

I was whipped.

Eventually, I dragged myself out of bed and into the shower. Val, Adam, Pepper, and the guys greeted me in the dining room.

"Why are you up so early?" I directed the question to Ezra and Ryder.

"Going into the office before class," Ryder said.

"Mom wants me to swing by the restaurant. She's throwing a correspondents' dinner in three weeks and this morning is the only time Chef has to finalize the menu." Ezra swiped a finger of cream off his pancakes and put it on Val's nose without a break in speech.

She cried out—half laugh and half scream—and whipped her napkin at him. Ezra caught it one-handed, tugged it free, and gently wiped her nose. They shared a loving kiss. All forgiven.

"Now that I'm talking about it," Ezra continued. "Your dad is coming, right?"

"Why would my dad go to a correspondents' dinner?"

"Mom wants him to give a speech on cybersecurity. One of our competitors was hacked and they got the names of three confidential sources off their servers. She figures everyone will be interested in learning how to prevent that happening again."

Our housekeeper, Matilda, set a plate of strawberry-covered chocolate chip pancakes in front of me. Now that Caroline was in remission, she was indulging her appetite and the chef was cooking meals to satisfy.

"My dad won't say no to Amelia. If he wasn't ridiculously in love with Mom, I'd wonder if there were some suspiciously brown siblings in your future."

Ezra choked on his sip of tea. "Fu— Forget you," he corrected. "One Beaumont brother is more misery than I've earned in my life."

Our breakfast continued in the same charming vein. Sometimes I wondered about the example we were setting for Adam, acting like, well, twenty-one-year-olds. But the kid remained incorruptibly sweet day after day, and Val was always there to rein us in.

An hour later, we packed into our cars and headed off in every direction. Val and I dropped Adam off at school and then continued to the university.

"Nervous about the first day?" I asked.

"Nervous about classes? No. Nervous about my first batch of pledges? A little bit."

"Why?" My hand curled around hers. "You're the best president Zeta Rho has ever had."

"Am I? How would you know?" she teased.

"Everyone knows. It's all over campus. The secret's out."

Her soft, throaty laugh tugged a smile free.

"It's just more girls to coordinate. More activities. More events. And I have to be there for all of them because the final decision has to go through me. I can't accept or reject girls I haven't spent time with." She blew out a breath. "Let me say it now with you as my only witness, I'm so glad Blair is back. She's already taken over the planning for rush week. Blair set up the schedule for the orientation week booth. Also, she's begun talks with the Evergreen Country Club for our second annual charity dinner."

"Second annual? I thought you only threw the first to get your hands on the list of alumni."

"I did. Turns out my genius takes a life of its own. It was such a hit, they want to do it every year. I don't get to touch the guest list though," she added.

"It was a hit, babe. We raised the largest donation the food bank has ever received. You could alternate the charities you sponsor every year. Spread some of this Evergreen wealth to people who need it." My phone chimed. "One minute.

"Hello?"

"Rick." A deep, unmistakable baritone rolled out of my speaker. "You busy?"

"No. What's up, Aiden?"

What's up, Aiden?

It still struck me cold that I was on a first-name/nickname basis with the guy. He called me up. We played poker and partied every other weekend. It was becoming commonplace to see his number on my screen.

"Listen. The guys are all agreed that we want you in. Come to the field tonight. Midnight. We'll make it official."

"An empty field in the middle of the night? Do you know what number they clocked my IQ?"

Val squeezed my hand. *What's going on?* she mouthed.

He chuckled. "Meaning you're not stupid enough to come? After everything, you still don't trust us."

"You're forgetting I know how you initiate people."

"No one is going to make you spill your secrets in a basement, Rick. We do things differently in the club. If you want in, you'll be at the football field tonight. Alone. I'm serious about that last part."

Click.

"What happened?" Val asked.

I took a deep breath. "I realize that the next thing I say will cause you to want to come with me, but you can't, so let's get that out of the way."

"What are you talking about?"

"Aiden told me to meet them at the football field at midnight tonight. It's time for my initiation."

"I'm coming," she said predictably.

"He says I have to go alone."

"I don't give a fuck what he says."

"If we show up together, he'll forget the whole thing and not let me join. You know the guys are holding back with me. All they've done all summer is play poker, ask questions, and fool around. Surprisingly tame for the no-holds-barred club the book described. We can't know what Aiden's got them into until I'm in for real."

Val nodded along. "I'm hearing everything you're saying and it makes perfect sense, but here's the thing"—she cupped her hand around her mouth—"you're not going there alone! This guy *kidnaps* people. Six against one, Maverick. Even you would have trouble fighting them off."

"Valentina—"

"My love, if you didn't want me to flat-out stalk you, you shouldn't have told me where you'd be."

"I— But—" *Shit. Maybe I'm not a genius.*

VALENTINA

"Mai, what are you still doing here?" Blair cried. "You were supposed to start your shift at the booth five minutes ago."

Mai froze deer-in-headlights style. Olivia's homemade caramel pretzel brownies hung half out of her mouth. Mom wanted to support me on my first day of welcoming new pledges, so she tossed in some goodies to go with the treats we put out for the looky-loos.

They were supposed to be for the Zeta Rho hopefuls. Instead, they were heading down my sisters' gullets fast.

"I was just—"

"Go, Mai!"

She went.

I smothered a laugh as she grabbed her stuff and beat it out the door. I closed it behind her with a look to Blair. "I know you function on a steady drip of stress, but everything is going to be fine."

"Fine?" she repeated. "How can you say that? These will be the first new sisters since us. It's on our shoulders to pick the women who'll carry on our legacy. And do I need to tell you what goes into making that decision?"

"No."

"Extra bonding activities. Extra physical activities." Blair rattled it off like I hadn't spoken, fingers held up to illustrate. "We have to give them the test and take them to the obstacle course. You and I must keep eyes on them every second of every day to make sure our final ten are the girls who'll represent Zeta Rho. And the initiation," she burst out. "We're not spilling secrets which means we have to think of another final test for the girls."

"Blair." I touched her temples, massaging tiny circles. "Deep breaths. In and out."

"Be serious, Val," she snapped even while she slowed her breathing.

"Everything is going to be fine. You'll focus on the sisters and I'll take on the pledges. I'll book us the military obstacle course this week and for the initiation, we'll do a game-show-style event where the sisters put together everything they've learned.

"Intellectual challenges that test them on the charter and general knowledge. And physical challenges like a tightrope, hurdles, stepping stones, or belly crawls. I looked it up and we can set all that stuff up in our backyard. They gave us a bunch of extra money in the budget to host rush and pledges. We won't even make a dent buying the things I bookmarked."

"Oh. A game show." Blair took hold of my hands and pressed them together between us. She grinned at me over my fingers. "This is why they call you madame president."

"Actually, I've worked real hard to get them to *stop* calling me madame president," I teased. "Come on, Blair. You know I wasn't going to let you handle all of this by yourself. We split the work fifty-fifty like always."

She took a breath, held it, and let it out slow. "I know we'll be okay. It's just... all eyes are on us, Val."

"Eyes like whose?" I asked softly. "Your mom?"

Blair pinked. "She expects a lot from me. What mother doesn't? She won't stand for me not to live up to my true potential or for me to bring Zeta Rho down. Everything has to be perfect."

"Everything *will* be perfect. It's day one and we're all kicking ass. We've clearly got the best snacks on the row because *the sisters can't stop eating them*!"

Keily and Sofia jerked red-handed. Bold as shit, Sofia snatched the tray of caramel pretzel brownies and took off running.

"Hey!"

"Catch me and do something about it."

Blair glared at me. "This is what I'm talking about. The Sallys are about class and dignity. Who is going to take us seriously when our sisters are in the corner hoarding brownies like they're Gollums with the ring?"

It was hard to defend Sofia when she was upstairs cackling and taunting me. "Nice job landing that Lord of the Rings dig."

"Ugh!" Blair stomped off—no doubt to check, recheck, and check again that everything was perfect.

"Sofia Richards," I called up the stairs. "Stop torturing Blair. And give me back my brownies."

"Too late. They're gone."

I went up, catching a glimpse of her as she disappeared into her room. I walked in and flung myself on her bed. Sofia followed suit, jumping on top of me and laying her head between my shoulder blades.

"Blair has every right to be nervous," I said. "We struggled to the end of sophomore year, and this year we'll have even more on our plate. I should be feeling the same, but all I can think about is Maverick."

"Is he really going tonight?"

Sofia knew about Aiden's invitation. Of course she knew. There wasn't a single thing I didn't share with my best friend.

"He says he has to. The guys are holding back with him and the only way to find out Aiden's true goal is to lower his guard."

"Why does that mean he has to meet up with that creep in a deserted stadium in the middle of the night? Why can't Kendra, Teagan, Sabrina or Eve tell you what his true goal is? If they're really the friends they've been pretending to be all summer, you'd already know everything about the club."

"You have a point," I muttered. "But those four just keep telling me different versions of the same answer. The club is about pushing boundaries. It's about deeper bonds of sisterhood. Stretching ourselves to the limit of what we thought we knew.

"They say that, but when we go to their parties, all they do is hook up and lose money. Maverick might be right. We won't see any more until they consider him as one of them."

"Please tell me you're not letting him go alone."

"Hell no, I'm not." I flipped to face her. "We agreed I'd be there. Hiding."

She nodded. "Please tell me you're not thinking I'd let you crouch in the stands by yourself."

"Aiden demanded a midnight meetup to be extra creepy. You shouldn't have to drag yourself out of bed to—"

"Val."

I sighed. "Yeah, I know. We'll be up there hiding together."

"Yes, we will," she said, looking smug. "Bring more brownies in case it goes long."

MAVERICK

To say I was a tad distracted that day would be to say *Pan's Labyrinth* was kind of an okay movie. It's flipping brilliant, and I didn't hear a word in my Introduction to Nanoelectronics, Computational Cognitive Science, or Database Systems classes. I walked out of there with blank notebooks and judgmental headshakes from my professors.

I'm hours away from meeting a potential sociopath in an empty field. If he jumps me with his six buddies, my girlfriend will risk herself trying to save me and we'll both be taken and never seen again.

That explanation would've bought me some sympathy but I held on to it for obvious reasons.

After my final class, I slid into my car and set off for home. My first one.

Mom greeted me at the door with her newest accessory riding shotgun in her purse. Chester's furry head poked through the strap. He barked at me as if to say his current situation was my fault.

"So much for the Beaumont Boys being the animal lovers."

She clicked her tongue. "What can I say, I held him and fell in love. You were right. Samson and I are swinging by the spa to meet up with the girls."

"Samson? What was wrong with Chester?"

"Nothing's wrong with Chester, but he's going to be a big, strong boy and he needs a strong name. Won't you? Won't you, little boy?" Mom cooed at the pup, kissing all over his face.

I inched around her and hurried off. Once she was done with him, it'd be me next.

"Have fun at the spa, Mom."

"Bye, baby."

Bounding up the stairs, I searched for my father in his usual places. The library. *Empty.*

The sun room. *Not a soul.*

His office.

Dad glanced up from his paperwork as I strode in.

"I should have checked here first."

"Son." Dad rose up, arms out to envelop me in a crushing hug. My bones ground together when he hugged me. I could only imagine what it was like for smaller, daintier people. I.e., nearly everyone other than me.

"What brings you by?" he asked.

"Do I need a reason?"

Dad guided me over to the armchairs. The cool leather on my back swirled memories of long nights bent over the computer with my father. He'd let me run around unrestrained in here, going so far as to remove anything breakable or expensive so this could be my second playroom.

That was the lens through which I viewed the world. Sitting on the carpet with my toys and peeking up at my father—larger than life behind his desk. Smart. Powerful. Strong.

I knew at five years old that he was what I wanted to be when I grew up.

"You never need a reason, Ricky. So tell me, how did the first day go? How is the lovely Val and my boy Adam?"

We launched into the usual conversation, filling each other in on what went on in our short time away.

"Hope you're not busy in three weeks," I said. "Amelia's angling for you to give a speech at her correspondents' dinner."

"She sent me an email this morning. I'll be sure to follow up with her." Dad leaned back in his seat, scanning me up and down. "But you didn't come here to tell me what Amelia did herself. Something is bothering you, son. Out with it already."

I cracked a smile. "When I start off with the bad news, you ask why we can't have normal conversations anymore. When I open with the pleasantries, you accuse me of stalling. You're impossible to figure out, Dad."

"You're damn right, and that fact has kept me in business all these years. Now what's wrong, Rick?"

Dropping my head back, I turned my gaze on the vaulted ceilings to hide the indecision in my eyes. How much was I going to tell him?

"Rick?"

"Do you remember Ezra's accident two years ago?"

"The shooting? Of course I remember."

"No. Before that. Although, it is connected." I dropped my chin, locking on to him. "Remember when he fell chasing the van?"

"Ah, yes. The boy Ezra claimed was kidnapped." Dad rose and moved over to the bar cart. "Hasn't he made it home safe and sound?"

"He did, but it's not about Sawyer. It's about the guy who lured him to the van in the first place." I twisted to track him crossing the room to close the door. "Dad, tell me why someone would protect their hard drive with an S-one trifid encryption using a straddle algorithm."

"Trifid encryption?" He retook his seat and handed over a glass of scotch. "Protection like that, we're talking state secrets, banking information, or intellectual property worth billions. MT uses something similar to protect our proprietary information."

"Okay. Can you think of any reason why a college student—who isn't your son—would encrypt their files with trifid?"

Marcus inclined his head. "As I stated, he must have something highly valuable worth protecting. Encryption on that scale is not easy to achieve and it wouldn't be cheap to buy."

"Highly valuable was my first thought until I opened the file and found endless data on the men in the Nu Alpha Theta fraternity. Aiden has—"

"Hold on." Dad put up his hand, stopping me in my tracks. "Opened the file? You don't mean— Rick, did you hack this man? You swore to me you would never do that. I didn't teach you these skills so you could invade people's privacy."

"I didn't hack him. I became his poker buddy and he let me see the file."

The lie turned my stomach. I made a promise to my father and I took that sort of thing seriously. If I wasn't a man of my word, then what kind of man was I?

The answer is I'm the kind of man who'd do anything for the people I love. We had to know the truth about Aiden, the Sons of Slaughter, and just how much information he had that could bury us.

"He let you see it just like that?" Dad's eyes narrowed. "After the lengths he went through to protect it?"

"That's the thing. The file is just those stats, Dad. Height, weight, running times, eating habits, and social skills. I don't know what to make of it. Do you?"

"If he let you see his file, surely he explained."

"The fraternity. It's hard to get in and even harder to stay in. He tracks the brothers to see who is falling short."

The lines on his forehead hardened. "I see but... a trifid encryption."

"Ezra said he's dirty, Dad. It's looking more and more like he was right."

Dad tossed his head, face smoothing out. "Ezra said he was a kidnapper and the boy turned out to be fine. The encryption is a step above overkill, I will give you that. But have you considered someone who isn't my son may have the same skills with computers? He feels he has to collect this data and, apparently, he feels the same urge to protect it. Doesn't sound too dirty to me."

I rejected everything he said immediately. "You don't know what Aiden Connelly is like. Those all-knowing smirks. The hints he drops to Val. I trust Ezra's and Val's judgment."

"And I trust yours," said my father. "But I will say this, I've worked with many a former Sam or Sally. The fraternity has a strong reputation and the men it turns out go on to do great things. It's difficult to know the inner workings of a closed community like that, or say what practices are par for the course. It seems this Aiden Connelly is opening up to you. Give him a chance, Rick. Everyone deserves one."

"Could one argue he lost his chance when he threatened to tell the Sons of Slaughter where Brian was hiding?"

"One could," he admitted. "One could also recognize that in the end, he didn't get involved in the situation and what happened to Ezra was a result of you boys taking it on yourself to play undercover agents."

My head dropped right back on the chair. "Which we've apologized for a thousand times."

"Yes, you have apologized for hiding dangerous things from us, taking on a situation you weren't equipped to handle, going outside the law, and getting your best friend shot." A hand rested on my forearm. "You apologized and we forgave you, because chances aren't limited to one."

"All right, Dad." I placed my hand over his. "I get what you're saying."

Give Aiden a chance... to prove he's exactly what I think he is.

THAT NIGHT, OUR FAMILY sat around the dinner table eating ravioli with sundried tomatoes and pine nuts. On a normal day, that was my favorite meal.

I barely touched it.

My attention drifted to Val and, sitting by her side, Sofia. Neither one would hear of letting me meet Aiden alone. I had a niggling feeling that they were looking forward to sneaking around and pulling one over on him. I believed Aiden was a lot of things. Chief among them someone not to be underestimated.

After dinner, I carried Adam up to his new room. Daphne had out-done herself with a jungle theme—inspired by Val's trip to Costa Rica. Adam's walls were transformed into a window to another universe. Vines stretched over his canopy bed. Monkeys swung by his jungle gym and stuffed animals joined him in his reading nook.

Most nights he asked to sleep in the nook. That night was no different.

I tucked him into his makeshift bed of comforters, pillows, a snake, and two lemurs. Val watched from the doorway as we went through his routine. Checking the closet and under the bed for monsters, reading a story, and sitting tight until he fell asleep. Half an hour later, he was out like a light.

Val kissed me on my way out of the door. "It's a few hours until midnight," she said. "Sofia and I should get going."

"Now? Why?"

"I doubt he'll show up four hours early to shoot the shit. Sofia and I will find a spot to lie low, and when you arrive, you'll be *alone* as he demands."

Gripping her shoulders, I steered her away from Adam's room and propped her against the wall, staring hard into those flinty green eyes. "This is my last-ditch attempt to get you to stay here."

"Go for it."

"I love you and I promise nothing will happen to me. You trust me, don't you?"

Her lips quirked up at the edges. "I do, and well done whipping out the trust card."

"Thank you. I've got more."

"Please, continue."

"Aiden has no reason to come for me. I'm not a Sam and he knows I've got nothing on him. The book he gave you mentioned an initiation to get into the club. There's no reason to think this is anything other than what he says it is."

"The logical approach. I like it."

"One more."

"Let's hear it," she said.

"Sex."

"What?" Val burst out laughing. "Expound."

"Nonstop. Every sexual favor you can think of is yours on demand, and for this tempting offer, all you have to do is grab your best friend, head down to the theater and watch a couple of your favorites until I get back. What do you think?"

Val slid her hands up my shoulders, bringing me down to her height. Her kiss was a sweet gift on my lips.

"I think that I trust you absolutely but I don't trust Aiden or his friends. I think that just because an initiation is standard, it doesn't mean it's safe or something any sane person would choose to do. And I think all sexual favors are already available to me on demand." She popped another kiss on my cheek. "I heard your offer, considered it, and now it's time to go. See you soon, baby. I'll text you when we find a good spot."

With that, Valentina met Sofia at the top of the stairs and together they left. I considered going after her and then I considered I may be overreacting. The logic I gave Val held up. Aiden had no reason to snatch me off the street or murder me in a deserted field.

This is exactly what Aiden says it is.

CAMPUS WAS OPPRESSIVELY quiet. First night of school, and this late, students hadn't reached the point of slacking off. Drinking on shadowed park benches or searching for somewhere to hook up that wasn't five feet from their roommates.

No. All the good little Somerset kids were safely tucked in their beds. And I was alone.

I arrived at the stadium and a locked gate.

Me: I'm here. How do I get in?
Aiden: East entrance service door. It's open.

Ever been in a football stadium at night? No. Why would you? Why would anyone wish to enter the place like this? Forgotten echoes of cheering fans whispering through the gloom. Flickers out of the corner of your eyes that turn out to be another trick of a mind searching for someone. Anyone. And the sole beings those eyes find are six still figures in the middle of the field. Waiting for you.

Far enough away, I chanced a look where Val and Sofia were hiding. Section 22A. Ducked behind row 12. They got in without a problem and assured me Aiden and the guys didn't suspect a thing when they arrived.

"Maverick."

Aiden dropped his hood. He gave me a smile that didn't reach his eyes as he folded his hands in front of him. He adopted the same pose as the men standing silent. On his left side, Winston and Nasir fanned out. Rowen, Sawyer, and Hayes stood on his right.

Slowly, I clapped, drawing their eyes up their foreheads. "Well done. You're missing the hooded robes and burning torches, though. Might've pumped in some eerie music for the full effect."

"Funny," Aiden said tonelessly.

"Why am I here?"

"You know why you're here," Winston spoke up. "It's time you became one of us."

"Just how do I do that? Got another question for me. You looking for a rematch, Aiden?"

That same empty smile only grew. "A match is right, but not in football."

Before I opened my mouth to ask what that meant, his hands flashed. Aiden unzipped his jacket and tossed it. Crossing his arms, he grabbed the hem of his shirt.

"Whoa," I cried. "Let's keep our clothes on."

"I would," Aiden said, "but I like this shirt." He stripped it off and shoved it on Rowen. "Wouldn't want to get blood on it."

My hands curled into fists. That sickly amused smile was spreading, lighting on the others' faces. My expression was blank as I said, "Whose?"

"Yours if I'm as good as I think I am. Mine if I'm not."

I surveyed them, and then cast a quick look up at the stands. "You brought me here to fight."

"Ding, ding, ding," Rowen mocked. "He's got it."

"Why?"

Aiden threw out his hands. "What have we been saying all summer, Rick? If you want something, you have to fight for it with everything you've got. Anything less and you deserve to have it taken away from you. Every new recruit has gone against me on this field and only one has beaten me." Aiden cut eyes to Sawyer. "Caught me with a kick to the head that put me out for four hours. That's what it takes, Maverick. No Mercy."

I should've been surprised. Admittedly, I wasn't thinking fight club, but still, I knew he didn't bring me out here to blow bubbles and hold hands dancing in a circle. What truly worried me was Val's reaction when it started going down.

"So no rules?" I asked.

Nasir stepped forward. "No eye-gouging, hair-pulling, crotch shots, or shit like that. Otherwise, yes. No rules."

"All right, then that brings me to my final question. Why in the fuck would I fight you to get into this club? I'm not in your fraternity. I don't need poker money, and while the ladies you trade off sleeping with are lovely, I've got a lady of my own. You have nothing to offer me."

Moving back, I tipped an imaginary hat to them. "Goodbye, gentlemen. It's been fun."

"Wait," Aiden snapped.

"For what?" I turned my back on them. My phone was already in my hand to text Val to leave.

A flash streaked across my vision. Aiden planted himself in front of me. "Don't be so hasty, Beaumont. I can offer one thing that would be of interest to you."

I lifted my shoulders. "And that would be...?"

Leaning in, Aiden put his head by my ear. "The truth," he whispered. "The complete, honest truth behind why I collect the information in that file you've been snooping in for weeks."

My bones turned to lead.

He tsked. "You can't be surprised? Didn't you think the guy capable of creating that encryption would devise multiple methods of warning if it's ever broken? I should be pissed but, honestly, I'm impressed you hacked me in the first place. You're smart, Rick, and you've got balls. That's what I'm looking for."

Aiden stepped back. The smirk he shot me this time was real. "If you want to know why, you'll accept."

My breaths came in strangled pants. Sharp pinpricks of pain radiated from my palm. I dug my nails in harder to anchor me in the shock.

Aiden was onto me. Likely from the very beginning. He knew the entire time I've been after the truth about him and now he's offering to give it.

Why? Why when he has nothing to lose either way?

"Why?" I rasped.

"Because I'm getting pretty tired of you and your girlfriend—who I'm sure is somewhere nearby—treating me like a psycho killer. If you become one of us, there'll be no need to conceal the truth and we can finally put this behind us."

"And if I lose?"

"I don't tell you shit." Aiden's eyes narrowed to slits. "And you stay out of my business. Do we have a deal?"

I resisted the urge to look for Val again. With every muscle straining to stop me, I raised my hand and grasped his.

We shook.

"Deal."

VALENTINA

"Why in the hell is Aiden taking off his shirt?" Sofia hissed. "It's not *that* kind of initiation, is it?"

"What kind?" I shifted, jiggling my numb foot.

She shoved my shoulder, nearly dropping me on my ass. "Come on, Val. You've seen porn with the best of them."

I choked. "I have not!" My whisper-shout bounced around the empty space. "At least I haven't seen any where a bunch of dudes lure my boyfriend to a football field and have their way with him."

"That's called a gang bang."

"Behave or go to the car."

She clapped a hand over her mouth to cover her giggles. I was glad she was enjoying herself because two hours in and I was cursing Aiden and wishing Maverick told him to stuff his initiation down his throat.

Stuck between the rows and balancing on the balls of our feet to prevent our bodies from coming in contact with the myriad of unknown substances, was not how I wanted to spend my night.

We slipped in to wait without a hitch. The guys arrived together a half an hour before midnight and gathered in the middle of the field. The entire time they were locked in an animated six-way conversation. I would've given anything to hear what they were saying, but Sofia and I stayed put. Whatever they wanted from Maverick, we were here to back him up.

But he will be fine. They have no reason to hurt him. And they have no escape if they do.

I peeked over the seats, gazing down at the guys. Aiden and Maverick looked to be talking. Suddenly, Maverick spun on his heels and walked away.

"Sofia, look," I whispered. "I think Aiden laid out his offer and was shut down."

"Course he was." Our cheeks touched peering at the scene. "Maverick would never cheat on you."

"You're hilarious, but I didn't bring you here for comic relief."

"Seems like we didn't need to come at all. Maverick is leav— Wait. Look."

Aiden ran in front of him. I squinted as he got in my boyfriend's face. "What's going on?"

Maverick stepped back, and before our eyes, ripped off his shirt.

"Okay, no joking, Val. What's going on here?"

Rowen, Nasir, Winston, Hayes, and Sawyer surrounded them. Confusion burned in my gut until Maverick raised his fist.

"Oh no. They're going to fight!"

I shot to my feet. Sofia leaped and grabbed me, wrestling me back down. "Val, you can't."

"What do you mean I can't?!"

"Maverick's been throwing two-hundred-pound dudes across the field since high school. He can handle himself and he must think so too or he would've kept walking."

"I don't care. I'm not letting him get hurt over a situation he's in because of me."

She tightened her hold. "He's in this situation because of Aiden and Sawyer and now he's got a chance to find out what's really going on with both of them. We came here to protect him. Not to blow that chance."

"Sofia—"

"Maverick will be fine," she said firmly. "Now duck down before they see you."

I was torn between doing as she said and shoving her off and making a run for it. In the end, she was right about one thing. Maverick wouldn't be down there squaring up to Aiden if he didn't know he could take him.

"I'm stopping this the minute this goes too far," I warned.

"I'll be right there backing you up."

Down below, Aiden lunged. My breath stuck in my throat as Maverick ducked the first punch. He stayed light on his feet, moving around Aiden to keep him twisting for his target. Aiden lunged again and Maverick pivoted, seized his wrist, and flipped him.

The onlooking guys remained motionless as their leader struck the ground.

I released a breath. "Let that be the end of—"

Aiden shot up and tackled him. Both guys fell, grappling in the dirt, and striking with a ferocity I physically felt. Maverick elbowed Aiden across the jaw and once again the boy went flying.

"Told you he could handle himself." Sofia squeezed my hand. "What was Aiden thinking choosing a physical challenge for Maverick? Should've asked him to try to shove into those kiddy tunnels on the playground. Our boy would be straining to get his head and one shoulder in."

I chuckled softly, tension loosening. Maverick was handing his ass to him. He was fine.

The boys squared up once more. I wished I could see Aiden's face and if it was still twisted by that smirk.

Aiden broke the dance and ran straight at Maverick. My love crouched and used his opponent's momentum to devastate his blow to the stomach. Aiden collapsed on top of him and was flipped once more, striking the ground behind him. He didn't get up.

"Thank goodness," I breathed. "It's over. We can—"

Maverick stood to walk away. In the space of a blink, Aiden came to life, kicked out, and swiped him off his feet.

Maverick fell, and before he could rise, Aiden jumped on him, shoved him down, and punched him once, twice, three, four times in the face.

Sofia clamped down on my mouth as the scream ripped from my throat.

Aiden flipped him face-first in the dirt. Maverick didn't move to fight while his arm was wrenched up his back and his head was ground even further into the mud.

Maverick didn't move at all.

I wrenched free of her grip and raced through the stands, screaming his name.

Chapter Eight

Maverick
"Help him up, guys."

Hands grabbed my shoulders and arms, dragging me off the ground and out of my daze. My face throbbed like a meat tenderizer had been taken to me. Wetness ran down my chin, nose, and lip. I had a chance to glimpse the blood pool beneath me before I was turned over and dropped on my ass.

"Not bad." The appreciative drawl pierced my fog. "You got more hits in than I expected."

Aiden slowly came into focus—as did Val's screams. A red trail pouring freely from his scalp shone stark on his skin along with the grin that said he didn't care. He wasn't the only one. Rowen, Hayes, and the other guys all smirked at me like I'd just performed a cute trick.

"I'm gonna get out of here before your girlfriend takes another shot at kicking my ass." Aiden laughed. "In her case, I have no doubt she'd win." He clapped a hand on my shoulder. My swipe was too sluggish to stop him. "See you Friday night, Rick. Welcome to the club."

"Wh— What?" I croaked. "What the fuck? I lost."

"So? I said if you lost you'd stay out of my shit, not that you wouldn't get into the club. Friday night," he repeated.

The boys filed off, leaving me to sink onto the ground, slipping peacefully into blackness. Val's voice sought to bring me back. I let go of her... and everything else.

"MOMMY'S REALLY MAD," Adam said conversationally.

"You're telling me."

Valentina had been coming in and out of the room to shout at me for the last three hours. Ever since the doctor signed off on a clean bill of health. With the worry gone, the anger came flooding in. The second day of school and the two of us were home dealing with the aftermath of my *initiation*.

Adam ducked into our room halfway through to burrow into my side. I think he was also trying to comfort me in the wake of her onslaught.

"It's okay, Daddy." He patted my head. "Mommy will forgive you."

"Thanks, son."

He cocked his head, taking in the collection of bruises, cuts, and swollen skin that used to be my pretty face. "What happened?"

"Daddy got beat up," I said bluntly.

Adam gasped. "Someone beat *you* up? How?"

"There's always someone stronger, smarter, and quicker. The trick is for that person to be you. This time I wasn't."

His face crumpled in confusion. To be fair that wasn't the best explanation for a six-year-old.

"Daddy turned his back on the bad guy and he got me."

"Ooh," Adam said. "Don't do that next time."

"I won't. Believe me, I'll never turn my back on this guy again."

"—idiotic things I've ever seen!" Val blew inside. "Why didn't you walk away and *keep walking*? Why did you agree to fight him? Huh? Huh?!"

"I'm sorry, Val." Groveling was my only hope at this point. I tried pointing out earlier that it worked out and I'd gotten into the club. She glowered so fiercely, she singed my eyebrows.

"It was dumb. No argument here."

"Adam, find Chef in the kitchen. He's got a bowl of ice cream with your name on it."

"Yay!" He raced off and I was left to fend for myself.

"What kind of initiation was that?" Val climbed up and cradled my head on her chest. "He drags you out there, says he knew the whole time we got into the file, offers to come clean if you win, and then beats you and lets you into the club anyway? What was the point?"

"The point was to tell us who's in control, Val. And it's not us."

"Don't say that." She held me tighter. "We are in control. Aiden hasn't beaten me, and he hasn't beaten you. But... all this club stuff... it's time to put a stop to it."

"I'm finally in the club. I can't back out now that we might get somewhere."

"We're not getting anywhere like this. Hanging around him and hoping he spills the truth out of the kindness of his heart isn't going to work."

"It's not about him anymore," I argued. "Aiden whispered my prize for winning like he didn't want the others to know. Or at least one person in particular—Sawyer. I still say he's the way in. He's the one who has to tell us the truth of his disappearance, and he'll open up to me now that his president has welcomed me into the club."

"I'm sick to death of this fucking club! Seeing the people I love get hurt. Wondering if we'll ever really be safe. Seeing Leighton ghosts everywhere I go! I regret every day that I joined that fucking sorority."

Threading my fingers through hers, I placed our hands over my chest. Hers rose and fell with hard pants, but slowly, her heart thrummed it's melodic, steady beat.

"You don't regret it," I said softly. "You love being president. Those women have become like your family and you care about them. You care if someone is trying to take advantage of them. We don't know what Aiden is up to but he stopped pretending he's innocent. I'll get the truth about the files even if I have to do it another way."

"I just don't know w-what this is all for anymore." Her voice cracked. "Sawyer and Teagan party with this guy every other week.

They're clearly not victims. What Ezra overheard in the basement wasn't what we thought it was—like Aiden's said the whole time. As for Leighton and Logan, the friends who covered up his death had to do with her and her alone. It's not connected to Zeta Rho."

"How does that explain the people who've gone missing from the Sam and Sally house for years? Or your housemother's reaction every time you suggest that something isn't right?"

"What if I don't give a shit anymore?" she snapped. "Sofia and I half-carried you to the car last night. I'm done, Maverick."

I fell quiet, choosing my words carefully. "If you're done... then be done with all of it, Val."

"What does that mean?"

"Drop out of the Sallys." Rising up, I met her shock head-on. "All of this started the day you walked into that welcoming reception. It only ends when you walk out."

"But, Maverick—"

"You can't think I'll sit back and stick my head up my ass while Aiden, Sawyer, Teagan, Eve, and the rest of them continue lying straight to your face. We don't know the truth behind what Aiden did to Sawyer but the only person who hasn't lied in all of this is Ezra. Aiden did something to that guy and it doesn't matter if he won his forgiveness. While that duplicitous bastard is right next door, I don't want you anywhere near the Sallys. What do you say?"

Val pressed her lips together, eyes wide. She didn't find a response, and she didn't have to.

I lightly kissed her cheek. That was all my busted lip could handle. "I thought so. You can't abandon your sisters any more than I can turn a blind eye to the suspicious things that have gone on in those houses. If Teagan's and Sawyer's year off was as innocent as they claimed, then all they have to do is tell the truth.

"Because we know the stories they've been spreading are bullshit. Let Aiden, Sawyer, or Teagan give us one straight honest answer and then this can be over. Until then, you're not fending for yourself with a bunch of people who lie as easily as they show their teeth."

"I just want this to be over," she whispered.

"Then let's end it." I cupped her cheek and kissed her—pain be damned. "Together."

VALENTINA

"Trust me, ladies and gentlemen, I sympathize. The test has beaten down even the strongest of us. Just do your best."

"Because if you don't," Aiden added, "you shouldn't expect to become one of us."

I glared at him over a sea of shocked whispers and wide eyes. He winked back.

A month had passed since this piece of crap beat my boyfriend unconscious. Mercilessly, life insisted on moving on and piling homework, classes, tests, and pledges in the process. It was a good thing I liked my bunch of pledges.

Ellie graduated top of her high school class. I credited the stellar education for her graphic, inventive swears that streamed steadily from her mouth during physical activity. Despite this, she didn't give up or ask to slow down.

Maeve could give Blair a run for her money in the type-A department. She was exactly fifteen minutes early to pledge events and she took every chance she got to tell me how much she wanted to be in her older sister's former sorority. Another Blair in the house would've given me pause if not for Mini-Blair's love of cooking. The two of us enjoyed more chats than I could count while standing at the island and whipping up something delicious.

Blakely forced me to recall the conversation I had with Aiden in his basement the year before. Pledges that went out of their way to connect with the sisters deserved extra points and, in her case, I agreed. Blakely was first to volunteer to help with events. If it was anyone else, I'd say they were kissing ass hard. But it was obvious to me Blakely truly liked hanging out with us, and everyone liked her too.

They were just three out of the amazing girls we chose to pledge our house. I honestly didn't know who I'd pick at the end of this.

Maybe this is why they came up with weeding challenges like the test.

I looked around at the wide-eyed, hair-tugging fidgeters who had only one minute until starting the test. I understood why we used this to narrow down the final pledges, but this test was still cruel and un-usual punishment.

I tugged Aiden out of the dining room. "We're not seriously drop-ping pledges based on their score, right? It's impossible to pass that thing. Leighton Lewis excluded for the wunderkind she was."

"It's up to you to decide the cut-off score," he said. "Remember the point is to see how they think and, most importantly, if they push through or give up when it gets tough."

"Fine."

I made to return to the dining room. Thinking better of it, I twisted around and buried my fist in his gut. He stumbled but didn't drop.

"Dammit, Val," he grunted. "Got it out of your system yet?"

"I'll let you know when."

I made it clear to Aiden a month ago that I'd punch his face in for as long as I was mad about Maverick. He laughed at the time, thinking I was kidding.

I wasn't.

My burning loathing notwithstanding, Aiden and I had been working well together in planning joint activities for the potential brothers and sisters. Now that Maverick and I were in the club for real, the keeping him at arm's length had to stop. Every other Friday when we got into the car to attend another party, I wished we refused to join.

I wished we ended it and moved on like I wanted to after the initi-ation.

I wished Ezra never heard that whispered conversation in the basement.

I wished I dropped the snacks, took Sofia's hand, and marched us out of that welcoming reception three years ago.

We wanted to uncover the secrets of Nu Alpha Theta and Zeta Rho Sigma and this is what we got. The old adage was true—be careful what you wish for.

"We'll see you at the party this weekend, yeah? Hayes's place this time."

"Can't wait."

"Hmm. Do I taste a tang of sarcasm?"

"Did you have to say it like that?"

He laughed. "No one is forcing you to come, Val. Stay home with the kid, cat, and puppy. Know what, now that I'm saying it, I think it's exactly what you should do." The laugh lines vanished. "We're getting pretty tired of you guys standing in a corner. The club isn't for spectators. Don't bother showing up."

I felt another punch coming. "You didn't beat my boyfriend just to turn around and kick us out. We will be there, and you want to know why?" I swallowed the scant distance between us. "Because I'm going to be everywhere you are until the day you finally leave this campus. In and out of Greek Row. I'll be at your parties. You'll see my specter in your fogged-up bathroom mirror. I'll even pop into your dreams. I'm not easing up until you tell me everything, Aiden."

Aiden bared his teeth. "What else is there to know?"

"I understand what it is you, Nasir, Rowen, and your buddies are really about. I know what you're all determined to hide, and after seeing the things you get up to, it's not a stretch to believe you'd be into darker stuff. I want to know where the file fits into your plan," I said, "and why *they* had to take Teagan and Sawyer."

"We agreed the cost of getting in the club was staying out of my business."

"You and Maverick agreed," I corrected. "You and I don't have that deal."

His sharp breath skated over my nose. "I've told you over and over again that it's not what you think."

"If you're innocent—"

"No, let me ask a question. Why haven't you considered that the secrets I'm keeping aren't mine to tell? You want to know what's going on in Sawyer's and Teagan's lives, ask them." He sidestepped me. "See you in the bathroom mirror."

That night, I kicked back on the couch with two blue heelers and a stack of test papers. "No one tells you how many late nights you're taking on when you sign up for this president gig, girls. Want my advice, stay out of the life."

Bitsy and Pepper cocked their heads in tandem. The puppies were growing fast and becoming more alike as time went on. Pepper was lucky her sister hung around after her brothers found their homes. Just like I was lucky my mom wasn't in a rush to leave.

"Kid." Mom walked in bearing two mugs wafting steam. "Hot chocolate break."

"My favorite kind."

Mom handed me my mug and budged up between me and the dogs. "What are you working on?" She read the first question. "Advanced mathematics for psychology? I didn't realize your curriculum was this intense."

"Not mine," I replied. "The pledges. It's the second big test to weed them out. The first is not remembering random details from the charter at a moment's notice. The third is being an unlikable bugger or falling short in the tasks. The final is the obstacle course. After all that, I choose my final six and they take their chance on my game show."

"Goodness. Sororities have changed since I went to school," she muttered. "Though, I'll be able to find out firsthand now."

I stilled. "What? Mom, are you serious?"

She beamed. "I did it, kid. As of today, your mother is a student of Evergreen Community College."

I would've hugged the crap out of her if we weren't holding scalding hot cocoa. "That's amazing. I'm so happy for you. Does this mean...?"

"No," she said gently. "I've already started looking for a place near the campus."

"But Caroline said—"

"I will be forever grateful to Caroline for everything she's done for us, but it took me a long time to get here, Val. Strong. Independent. I'm not ready to give that up yet." She put her arm around me. "I'm also not interested in being hours away from my family. The community college is a half-hour drive. We won't see each other any less."

"I am happy for you, Mom. I'll miss having you right down the hall, but nothing has to change if we don't let it." She kissed my cheek. "What will you study?"

"I'm finishing my degree and then taking it one day at a time from there."

"Love that plan." I patted my stack of papers. "Whatever you do, don't join a sorority."

She bumped my shoulder. "You say that but every other weekend you're out having a good time with your friends. You needed this," she said. "High school wasn't the experience it should have been for you. It's such a relief to me that you're having fun in college." She tapped my homework. "Your present situation excluded."

My smile tightened around the edges, holding with difficulty. "Yep. I'm having so much fun, Mom."

"YOU DON'T HAVE TO DO this."

Maverick cut the engine. Music poured out of the mansion, welcoming us inside. We ignored its call in favor of sitting in the dark.

"Let me take you home."

"Remember the deal." I traced the shell of his ear. "We'll find the truth together. If we stop, we do that together too."

"You don't want to be here, Val."

Friday night arrived and along with it our invitation to Hayes's house. Maverick's GPS hung between us, congratulating on successfully arriving at our destination.

That thing is happier about being here than we are.

"Aiden can tell that too." The intricate white and gold Venetian mask mocked me. Empty eyes pierced my soul, and swallowed it as I secured it on my face. "No more standing in the corner."

"We're not doing half the shit they do."

"Then we'll do the other half." I opened the door. "Put your mask on, love. It's time."

Maverick fell in with me on the front stairs. Lacing our fingers together, he placed them over his heart, soothing me like so many times before.

I reached for the knob. It flew away and a wall of sound rushed out, bowling us over.

"Rick! Val! Finally." The long hooked nose of the pantalone mask nearly poked my eye out as Rowen grabbed and threw his arms around us. The resemblance to the mask worn by old plague doctors wasn't lost on me. Part of me wondered if he chose it on purpose.

"About time you got here," he said. "We got something special for tonight. Just for you, Val."

"What's for her?" Maverick demanded.

"Can't tell before the big reveal." That he was enjoying himself was as clear as the gaudy reds and golds of his mask. "Come on. We're in the ballroom."

"A ball? Is that why we're wearing these ridiculous outfits?" I asked.

I glanced down at the gold tulle beaded gown. My dress flared at the waist, spreading out in all directions and preventing me laying my arms flat by my sides. I looked like I could conceal three more of me under this thing.

Maverick, on the other hand, was a lordly rogue. The cloak, gloves, and leather hat danced with fantasies in my mind.

"Nothing ridiculous about you in that dress, Valentina."

Maverick snarled low in his throat. "Is the next thrill you're chasing being put through that fucking wall, Burke?"

"Oh ho," he laughed. "Just an innocent compliment."

Rowen marched us further down the hall. The music grew to deafening. In spite of our wardrobe, a loop of rock, pop, and rap thumped the speakers—so loud the chandeliers rattled over our heads.

Hayes's home was and *wasn't* what I expected for the kingdom of a health food conglomerate. I pictured an ode to life in green motifs, plants, and vibrant paintings of forests and animals.

I got the forest at least. Black-and-white birch trees adorned the walls, plunging us in a world without color.

Nearly everything was gray, black, white. Black lamps. White chandeliers. Gray doors with white bucking stags locking horns where the wood met. Rowen pushed through and swept us inside.

I stopped dead on the threshold, thinking for a second my mind was playing tricks on me.

Colors swirled on the dance floor. Scarlet satin whispered past cream chiffon. The click of gold heels and tinkling jewels might not have been heard over the music if not for the hundreds sounding in unison.

"Who are all these people?" I shouted.

"We put out a last-minute invitation around campus to whoever could swing the dress code. We figured why not?" He gave us a little shove. "Go. Dance. Drink. Val, they'll get you when we're ready for you." Rowen's wink sought me through the mask.

"Ready for what?" Maverick bellowed at his retreating back. He swore. "Val, forget this shit. We're going now."

I opened my mouth to argue and found myself swept off my feet. Maverick tossed me over his shoulder, carrying me out of the ballroom.

"It's a test, Maverick," I said to his back. "You had yours and now I have mine. I pass or I'm out."

"These people are insane." He plopped me on my feet. "Whatever they've thought up for you, you're not doing."

I quirked a brow. "Surely that's my choice."

"You're mistaken."

I couldn't help but smile. Can't lie. More than a few times their overprotectiveness drove me nuts. Putting tracking apps on my phone for example. But most days—actually, every day when they showed up exactly when I needed them, I loved them deeper for how much they loved me. "It'll be okay. They're insane but they don't have death wishes."

"Not entirely sure that's true. Two weeks ago, it seemed a slow painful death was exactly what they were after."

Wincing, I tried to think of a rationale and came up short. "I miss the days when they were holding back."

"But they're not anymore." Maverick cast a look around. Taking my hand, he pulled us into a nook between the wall and bookshelf. "We didn't understand why the lies, or disappearances, or Aiden's permanent shit-eating smirk. Now we do."

"We're only guessing," I whispered.

"It's a pretty good guess. The reason for all of this is—"

"Rick?"

I jumped.

"What the hell are you doing, man? Your tree-trunk self can't hide behind—" Hayes stepped into view. "Ah." He winked at me. "If you want to hook up, any room upstairs is yours. I know you like your *privacy*."

It's the world I walked into where not getting naked with my boyfriend in front of an audience was said with disdain.

"Thanks," I said lightly. "We'll take you up on that offer."

"Grab a drink with us first. Loosening you up before the big event."

Us came around the corner. Eve, Sabrina, Winston, and Phillipa got their hands on us and we returned to the ballroom. Through another lens, the party was magnificent. They leaned into the grays and blacks, weaving fairy lights around the room and setting up silver glitter machines that rained down on the guests. The shouting, gyrating, drinking, and cheering pointed to this being named the best party of the year.

Maverick and I drifted one way and the others went left toward the long table bearing drinks. It was impossible to tell who anyone was behind the masks. I assumed they were Somerset students, but who knew what circles the club members ran in.

"Whoo!"

Another cheer pierced the music. Maverick peered over the bobbing heads.

"Something's going on," he shouted. "There's a crowd in the middle of the dance floor."

It did appear the dancers were converging on one place. Curious, I pushed through the bodies with Maverick on my heels and then with him in front of me, shifting people aside with that hulking mass of muscles and perfection.

I stuck to him to avoid the pushy, braying dancers. They were shoving like it was a mosh pit and the song playing, "Freaking Me Out" by Ava Max, was catchy, but not a head banger. The drinks were clearly flowing freely tonight.

Suddenly, he stopped, bouncing me off his back.

"Maverick?" I yelled, but he couldn't hear me. The whooping and shrieking were even louder. A break appeared between the bodies and I spotted white marbled floor. Lifting his arm, I finally saw what everyone was looking at.

Sawyer flew at Aiden. Hooking his arm around his neck, he dropped and both boys smacked the marble hard, ripping grunts out of both of them. I didn't know how long they'd been at it, but their tattered shirts, ripped breeches, and blood gushing from various cuts on their faces and bodies said it was long enough.

Aiden sunk his elbow his Sawyer's gut, loosening his grip and using the chance to deal the sinking blow. Blood spurted from Sawyer's ruined nose.

A month ago, I would've run into their arena and broken up the fight. Raged at them for acting like stupid brutes and put them in separate corners until they decided to work out their issues civilly.

What I did instead was look around for Nasir, Hayes, or Winston. Surely one of them was taking bets.

Because that's what the club is about. The guys doing what they want, when they want, and making a lot of money in the process.

Money. Or cars. Drugs. Girls. Favors. The list didn't end and neither did the twisted challenges these guys came up with. The Friday before last, Nasir used the connections only a rich man could have and rigged a tightrope on the beach. Pretty tame until you set fire to the bed of coals beneath it.

I thought there was nothing left in this world to shock me. But when Nasir bet Sawyer thirty grand to walk the tightrope, risk second-degree burns and disfigurement, my jaw dropped. When Sawyer agreed to cheers and crowing from his friends—girlfriend included—I turned and walked out.

Sawyer clearly survived his walk above the flames only to mess himself up in another fight with Aiden. They did this a lot—fight Aiden. Barring Sawyer scoring a lucky shot that got him into the club, Aiden was impossible to defeat.

Aiden caught Sawyer's fist, twisted it behind his back, and kicked the back of his legs. The taller boy went down howling.

I hope he's cursing the decisions that led to him on his knees before Aiden once again.

Aiden helped him to his feet. I saw them shake before the crowd swallowed them. The show was over. Back to partying.

A hand secured my wrist. "Val, we've got to go!"

Teagan followed shouting in my ear with tugging me between the couple separating us. I stumbled into her and the waiting arms of Eve and Sabrina.

"Let's go," Eve echoed. "They're waiting for you upstairs!"

"Waiting for me?" I twisted to find my love. "Maverick!"

"Leave him," Sabrina said. "He'll try to stop you."

I narrowed on her. "Why would he need to do that? What exactly is waiting for me upstairs?"

"Your initiation." Teagan's eyes were hard. "Do it or leave, Val. The choice is yours."

I hesitated.

I came this far to find the truth. Maverick could be right that we know all we need to now, but the twist to Aiden's enigmatic smile says there are a few more secrets to uncover... and I'll find out what they are tonight.

"Fine. Let's go."

Maverick didn't notice us leave. I know because he didn't throw bodies across the room coming after me.

Stepping out into the hall, the noise muted behind shut doors. Silently, I followed the women through the colorless hallway to a winding staircase.

I set foot on the tenth step and heard, "Val?"

Teagan picked up the pace, expecting me to do the same. Maverick was looking for me.

We reached the second-floor landing and turned to continue up.

"I know it's in the rules somewhere to layer everything in a double dose of creepy," I began, "but could we dispense with that this time and you tell me what's going on?"

"We did tell you," said Eve. "It's your initiation. You don't want a club for the Sallys—that's fine. If you're going to be in this one, though, you have to prove yourself same as everyone. You've dodged the other challenges. This one is just for you."

Sabrina squeezed my forearm. "You can do it, by the way. I'm dropping the creepiness to say you're badass and Aiden has no idea what he's dealing with."

The niggle of warmth broke through, reminding me sharply of the summer we had before it soured. "You guys really want this? To be a part of it? To have a club of our own? I get that it's a lot of money. I've been poor. *Poor* poor. Sleeping-on-a-street-corner poor. I haven't fallen so far into my new life that I've forgotten the girl who would've done anything to get her mom and son out of poverty. But is playing their games truly worth it?"

"We've all got our reasons for being here, Val," Eve replied. "Should we ask what yours are?"

I said nothing.

"Thought so."

I didn't attempt to appeal to them again as we topped the third landing. A hallway of closed doors greeted us—just as gray as the last.

Teagan led the way to the fifth entrance on the right. We tromped in and Hayes's voice reached me. I looked and didn't see him anywhere in the grand room. His mother's bedroom if the photos of a pretty woman and Hayes at various stages in his life was anything to go by.

"Ben," Eve called.

A head poked inside the room. Hayes waved from the balcony, signaling us to join. "Right out here, Val."

"What's out there?"

"See for yourself."

I stepped over the threshold and came face to face with three guys, two patio chairs, and a table. No one was wearing a mask. "This is it?" I asked. "The way y'all were going on, I expected a cocktail of loopy juice that would crack my mind and reveal my mission to save the universe."

Nasir laughed. "I do like you, Val. It's a shame you've capped your harem at four."

"Why does everyone call it that?" I muttered under my breath. Louder, I said, "What do I have to do?"

"It's simple." A soft trill slid into my ear, spinning me on my heels. Aiden stood half out of the shadows. The half I laid eyes on had a smear of blood on his cheek. "Get up on the balustrade."

"Excuse me?"

"You. Balustrade. Now." Aiden stepped into view. Under his arm, he carried a small bucket. "Please."

I looked at the stone balustrade wrapping around the balcony. Then I looked for wide eyes or opened mouths, and saw none.

"Are you serious? You expect me to climb up there and do what? We're three floors off the ground, Aiden."

"What's that saying?" Aiden brushed past me. "It's not the fall that kills you, it's the impact. Well, if you do neither, you won't have a problem, will you?"

"What the fuck are you going on about?"

"It's simple." Aiden parked himself on one of the chairs. "Think of it like that absurd game show you're planning for the pledges instead of the real initiation. You stand up there and I'll throw these"—Aiden pulled a ping-pong ball out of his basket—"to you. For each one you catch and hold on to, I'll ask you a question about Zeta Rho Sigma. If you catch and answer ten, you're in. Easy, right?"

I nodded, lips pursed. "Aiden, let me ask you a question? Are you out of your damn mind?"

He cracked a grin. "Figured you might have that reaction, but don't worry, the same rules apply. The pot must be appropriately sweetened before we ask you to do anything risky. Want to name your price?"

"I'm sorry, maybe I'm being too subtle. I'm not getting on that ledge, Aiden! You can shove your head in the fucking pot and suffocate in it!"

I turned to go and bumped into a fleshy wall made of Teagan, Eve, and Sabrina.

"Yee-ouch." As usual, Aiden was as relaxed as a spring day. "If you don't want to name it, I'll give you my offer. Get up on that ledge and I'll tell you the true purpose of the club."

"Fuck you."

"—and the truth about my file," he added.

"Fuck you twice," I spat. "In the mouth and up the ass. I won't do it."

He continued like there wasn't an interruption. "I'll tell you how I get my information."

"No."

"Teagan and Sawyer will reveal where they truly were during their *sabbatical*."

"N—" The automatic refusal lodged in my throat. After months, bordering on years of denial, Aiden casually dropped that on the table like it was nothing. I gaped at him, eyes sliding to Teagan, who nodded expressionlessly.

"No," I croaked. "I don't need to know where you've been to accept you were caught up in something bad. Maverick was right. The few weeks have told us everything we need to know. This is all some sick game. A game you didn't start, but one you've embraced. Twisted games have even worse consequences and whatever they were," I said to Teagan, "I'm done trying to help.

"I'm done with all of this," I said to my silent audience. "Finally, I'm going back to my life before Sawyer asked Ezra to help him with the keg. Good luck to you." I stuck my hands through Teagan and Sabrina and parted them like the Red Sea. I didn't spare a look back as I marched out.

Aiden was in front of me in a flash. I raised my fist prepared to *force* him out of my way.

"And my final offer," Aiden whispered, speaking for my ears only. "If you pass this initiation, I'll tell you about Leighton and Logan Bilius."

I froze.

"Come on, Val. We all know she isn't dead. At least, you and I do. Anyone that can disappear a body will know a few tricks to disappear herself. Want to know the truth about that night and who Leighton Lewis really is?"

"That's what I'm offering, Valentina," he said in a louder tone. "A prize of equal or greater value. The truth, whole truth, and nothing but the truth. And all you have to do is..."

"Step onto the ledge." I spoke so softly I hardly heard myself.

"Exactly. Never say we don't give fair compensation."

I swallowed hard. "How could you possibly know about Logan?"

His eyes flashed. "I know everything about that night. Down to the revenge your boyfriends enacted. It was elegant, I'll give you that. But if it was me, I would've killed those bastards and put their bodies somewhere they'd never be found. Leighton and I did make such a good team."

"Who are you?" I whispered.

Reaching over my shoulder, he pointed. "You know how to find out."

I didn't want to. My muscles screamed, tightened, and ached to stop me, but Aiden's growing smile told me they failed. I was walking onto the balcony... past Hayes, Rowes, and the girls... and up to the ledge. I peered over the stone, stomach dropping as though the unforgiving fall had taken me already.

"I catch ten balls and answer ten questions." The voice coming from my throat didn't sound like mine. "That's it."

"Catch and hold," Aiden replied. "Drop any and you get more questions thrown at you."

Nodding, I took off my mask and shoes. I paused a brief second to consider what Maverick would do if he came out and saw me up here.

He'd kill them. He would kill them all.

I threw my leg over and carefully got my feet under me. Standing up, I turned to face them. The ledge wasn't wide enough for me to stand securely. The top half of my feet hung clear over the balcony.

"Let's get this over with."

"Ladies," Aiden said. "Gentlemen."

The others went up to him and reached into the bucket. I went cold in understanding. They would all lob balls at me like a human target. I had to keep an eye on all of them, ready to grab a pong coming from any direction.

"Don't worry," Aiden said. "We won't be assholes tossing it high over your head or ten feet to the left. We play fair."

"Play," I spat. "That's your problem, Connelly. You still think this is a game."

He threw the ball at the end of my sentence. Quickly, I slapped my hands over it, catching it before my thighs. That simple movement rocked my foundation. I wobbled, heart leaping in my throat as another night and another ledge roared through my mind.

"The Sallys and Sams were founded in honor of who?" Aiden asked.

Only when I was steady did I answer. "Sally Hollenbeck." I shoved the first pong down my dress.

"Smart," Nasir praised in the midst of tossing his. I caught that one too—sans wobble. "What year were we founded?"

On it went. I dropped more balls than I caught. Eons passed and my bra held five. They stuck to their promise to throw them directly at me, but terror of knocking myself off-balance again stopped me from trying to catch most of them.

Hayes's ball sailed in a beautiful arch, dropping easily onto my cupped hands. "Nice," he said. "Who was president of the Sallys in 1990?"

"Blair's moth—"

"Val? Valentina, where are you?"

I nearly dropped the ball. Maverick's search of the mansion had brought him to the third floor.

"Val?" A beam of light swept over the carpet, growing as the door widened. "Are you in here?"

Maverick stepped into view. Our eyes locked and in the space of his jaw dropping, an explanation jumped to my lips.

"Next question," said Teagan.

A tiny plastic missile launched directly at my face. Instinctively, I jerked, hand flying to catch it, and the momentum knocked me off my feet.

"Maverick!"

Arms flailing, I tipped off the balustrade, plunging three stories to my fate below.

"Vaaaaal!"

Chapter Nine

Want to know what goes through your mind during a fall? Nothing.

Your heart leaps into your throat, strangling your screams, and stealing the few precious moments left you have to breathe. Terror blots your mind, forcing everything out but what your white-rimmed eyes see—what you left behind or what you're rushing to meet.

"Vaaaaaal!"

I hit the water with an unforgiving smack that tore another scream from me. The pool surged into my open mouth, determined to finish the job.

An arm encircled my waist, hauling me up. I burst to the surface shrieking and sputtering.

"You're okay, Val. I've got you," Sawyer said. "Aiden had us on standby in case you were desperate for a swim."

I was shaking too hard to smack him. Sawyer swam to the edge of the pool where Winston waited. With more gentleness than I credited these guys with, they lifted me out and Winston draped a towel around my shoulders. Maverick shouted at us through the entire ordeal.

"Val?! Val! Are you okay?"

"I-I'm okay."

"What happened?!"

I said the first thing that came to mind. "Aiden."

Sawyer wrapped me tighter. "Sure you're okay, Val? Kendra is close to your size. She brought you clothes to change into just in case."

"Just in case?" I repeated. "In case I fell three stories into a swimming pool!?"

"We—"

"Hey! Rick— Don't!"

A pained grunt and then something struck the water, dousing us all over again. Aiden burst out swearing, cursing, and flinging every obscene thought in his head at my boyfriend.

"Shit," Winston said mildly. "Is Rick going to toss them all over?"

"Just help me up."

The boys complied, getting me on my feet and even trading my towel for a dry one. I settled it on my shoulders as Aiden heaved himself out of the pool. "Is it even worth asking if you'll tell me the truth now?"

"Not worth it at all. You lost, Val, and the rules say you get nothing." He pushed past us, probably eager to get clear before Maverick came down. "And I always follow the rules."

I let him go. Aiden had told me plenty already. Leighton, Logan, and his knowledge of acts he couldn't know, but yet somehow did.

"Where are the change of clothes?" I asked.

"One of the bedrooms down the hall," said Winston. "We'll show you."

"Val!" Maverick barreled onto the porch. The glare he leveled at the boys who surrounded me burned them to cinders where they stood. "Fuck off!"

They fucked off. Backing away, they gave Maverick a wide berth.

"Second door on the left," Winston called to me.

I fell into Maverick's arms. He held me so tight, I felt he was trying to absorb me into his body where I'd never be hurt.

"Are you okay? Val, what were you doing up there?"

"Not here," I said softly. "Bedroom."

Maverick let me walk two steps and then swooped me up and carried me. I dropped my head onto his chest, breathing for what felt like the first time that night.

A black Peter Pan–collar dress awaited us on the bed. This room was nothing like the little I'd seen of the house. The blue and purple floral motif was reflected in nearly everything. The bedspread, the wallpaper, the carpet, and the armchairs beside the window.

Maverick placed me on the bed. My rogue disappeared before my eyes, shedding the gloves, cloak, and silly mask. Grasping my ankle, his movements were slow as he dried me.

"What happened up there, Val?"

"Aiden said he'd toss me a few balls and then tell me the truth about him, Teagan, Sawyer, the disappearances, Leighton, and... Logan."

He stilled. "Logan?"

"He knows, Maverick." Saying it out loud, it still didn't seem true. "Everything about that night and what you guys returned to do."

Maverick snapped his neck spinning on me. "What? How could he—"

"I don't know, and that's why I climbed onto that ledge. To find out."

He dropped onto the bed, still holding my leg. "Aiden knows that Leighton killed him?"

"And that she's still alive."

"Could it have been Aiden she called that night to clean up the body? Just who the fuck is this guy?"

"That was my question."

His gaze sharpened. "Finding the answer doesn't mean putting your life in danger, Valentina. Whatever that fuck dangled in front of you, you should've told him off and walked away. You chewed my ass out for getting in a fight with him. How was this any better?"

"I knew I'd fall in the pool," I tried.

"You can't swim!"

I winced. Maverick had every right to be angry with me. I went after him for participating in Aiden's twisted test and then I turned around and did the same.

"We pretend like we're fooling him," I whispered, "but the truth is Aiden's pulling all the strings in this puppet show." I pressed a soft kiss to his cheek. "I saw my chance to discover what's been haunting us since we set foot on that campus. My chance to end it like we swore we would. It seemed worth it—to go back to the way we were."

"We also promised to do it together." Maverick caught me as I reached for him. My eyes closed as he pressed my palm to his wildly beating heart. "Don't do that to me again."

"I won't."

"I had to throw a man off a balcony because of you."

A tiny snort escaped me. "No less than he deserved. Forcing me on a ledge and throwing ping-pong balls at me? Seriously, how does he come up with this stuff?"

"He's dangerous, Val." Maverick trailed his nose down my bridge and lightly nipped my lips. "If he's made anything clear tonight, it's that."

"I'm done. With Aiden. With the club. With Teagan and her lies. I've risked too much for someone who doesn't want saving." Maverick's lips caressed mine, borrowing a soft breath. "As for Leighton, I thought I was free of her when I threw away that knife, but in truth, she's been controlling me since that night. No more. But," I said as he pulled me to his chest. "I'm not leaving the Sallys."

"Val."

"I love it, Maverick. I love them." I lifted my shoulders helplessly. "My mom said she was happy I found my place in Somerset. That I had friends and was happy. I realized she was right. Those girls are my friends and despite Eve, Kendra, and Sabrina, I know that most of them are exactly who they say they are."

"How can I look the other way when that guy is right next door?"

"He's been right next door for a long time. Aiden isn't after me, and the people he is after are right there with him willingly. All we're doing at this point is entertaining him." I stroked his jaw. "Will you walk away?"

"I just saw you fall off a ledge, Val. You don't have to ask me if I'm done. I want nothing to do with these guys and they'll be glad of it. I don't know what I'll do the next time I get my hands on them. One of them should've said that it was wrong."

I shook my head. "It's not up to Eve, Nasir, or Teagan to be my voice of reason, but it is up to me when to say enough is enough." I slipped out of his hold, falling onto the sheets. "And I say enough with those guys crowding out our headspace. I don't want to talk or think about them." I lifted my foot. "I believe you were drying me, Mr. Beaumont. Please continue."

He smiled slightly. "Here? After everything."

"I can't think of a better time than following a near-death experience."

"Don't say that word," he hissed. "I may have to find Aiden's ass and throw him off again."

Gripping his lapels, I tugged him down. "Find my ass first."

Our lips clashed in a shower of sparks.

I reached for my buttons and Maverick stopped me. He rose—our lips staying connected until the last possible second. He towered over me, showering me in his pulsing, consuming gaze. Maverick said nothing. Merely twisted his finger.

I turned and got on my knees immediately. Gentle, calloused fingers encircled my neck, caressing a line over my collarbone and down the valley of my breasts. I held my breath unconsciously—excitement rising as he dipped into my bra and... drew back. I clicked my tongue on his hand's retreat.

"Tonight is not the night to tease me, Beaumont."

"The name is Maverick." He tipped my chin back, locking eyes. "I will hear that name on your lips. I'll make you scream it. Make you say it between your demands for harder, deeper, and more."

My throat bobbed against his fingers. Dampness collected in my soaked panties, begging for my sweet, gentle teddy bear to get filthier.

"This isn't a tease. It's a surrender."

What could be said to that, I didn't know.

Maverick dropped to his knees. One by one, he popped my buttons, dropping kisses on each inch of flesh they revealed.

"Up."

I never got on all fours so fast in my life—and I could do it pretty fast.

Maverick tugged my dress the rest of the way down, taking my thong with it. I lay naked, exposed, vulnerable before his mercy.

Hot breath blew over my pussy, curling my toes, fists, and even the hairs on my neck. "Please, Maverick."

"Please what?"

"Punish me."

He plunged inside and parted me easily with two fingers. His tongue found my clit, rolling and teasing the nub until my cries grew hoarse.

"Yes, please. Don't stop."

Maverick took his exploration up, tongue-fucking my weeping pussy to a chorus of moans. My orgasm was coming fast. Fisting the sheets, my back arched under the building pressure.

He pulled out.

"Maverick," I shrieked. "I very specifically told you *not* to stop."

"We're playing by different rules tonight, babe." A smack landed on my backside. "Turn over."

I nearly came right then. I flipped on my back, eager for more instructions.

Maverick flicked his eyes down. That's it. Just a roll of those hazel orbs.

Quickly, I undid his belt, flung it over my shoulder, and freed his straining length.

Maverick tangled in my hair, drawing my head back, and parting lips ready to receive him. He didn't ask and I didn't need him to. Maverick pushed inside, leaving a trail of precum on my tongue. He hit the back of my throat, going deeper than he normally did, and when he started pumping, that wasn't usual either.

Maverick fucked my mouth hard and merciless. My moans echoed around him, saying what I couldn't.

Harder and faster.

My hand slipped between my legs.

"Fingers where I can see them," he growled.

We can put denying me an orgasm on the list of firsts. Who is this man?

I gripped his ass instead, sinking my nails in his cheeks. He hissed and picked up the speed.

A bit-off curse and then salty-sweet cum filled my mouth. I swallowed every bit. Looking into his eyes, I swiped the stream running down my chin and licked my finger clean.

"Fucking hell, Val. Get up here."

I climbed him like a monkey, wrapping my arms and legs around him, gasping as he pushed the tip past my entrance. Maverick grasped my hips and slammed me up, down, up, down on his cock. My head dangled off my body, thrown back as I screamed with abandon. I didn't care who heard. I wanted everyone to hear.

I wasn't in control of this. Not of him or me or the cresting, crashing sensations dragging me to the depths. This wasn't sex. It wasn't lovemaking.

It was complete and absolute surrender to the man who owned me—heart, body, and soul.

My orgasm rushed to a crescendo, desperate for Maverick to hit the final note.

Gripping my hip, he lifted me up slightly and thrust, striking that spot with dead-on accuracy. I came so hard, shaking and screaming in his ear, I thought he'd drop me.

Which he did.

We both fell on the sheets in a sweaty, exhausted heap.

"Damn, baby," I gasped. "I thoroughly understand what it means to have the shit fucked out of me now."

He chuckled. "Does that mean you won't be climbing on any more balconies?"

"Well, if this is the result..."

Maverick finished undressing and tucked us under the sheets. Holding me close, he kissed all over my face and neck, my sweet bear returned.

"You spanked me," I said, teasing him. "Where did that come from?"

"Felt right in the moment."

"I hope it feels right in some of the moments coming up."

"I'm sure there will come a few occasions where you'll need to be punished."

The husky reply stirred my core for another go. But not here.

"Let's get out of here, love." I kissed him slow. "I want to explore this new sexual direction we're taking in our bed. And on our couch. And on our desk."

"Don't have to ask me twice."

It took a few tries, and a few more kisses, but eventually we dragged ourselves out of the borrowed bed and got dressed.

My hand firmly in his, Maverick and I left our safe haven, heading for the stairs. We made it to the first floor and passed through the way we came for the front door.

"Drop it."

"Back off, Aiden. You don't tell me what to do anymore."

"That's where you're wrong."

Their heated voices came out of the room ahead. I peered into a study. A white sofa set before a flickering fireplace—the single source of light in the room. Scanning for the boys, I landed on a desk, bookshelf, bar, and Aiden backing a red-face Sawyer into the corner. He shoved him and something hit the floor with a shattering crash.

"We had a bet and you lost. You want to end up back there, Burn?" I'd never heard Aiden use the tone he did right then. "Lose another year of your life? Just say the word."

"Hey!" I dropped Maverick's hand, running into the room. "What do you think you're doing? Get off of him."

Aiden twisted and glared a hole in me. "You know what? That's a great question, Val. What am I doing? If Sawyer wants to drink himself to death, why should I stop him?!"

"Watch yourself," Maverick snapped. "Don't talk to her that way."

I frowned. Aiden wasn't the yelling type, and Sawyer...

The taller boy turned his face from us, fist pale and balled at his side.

What's going on with these two?

"I will watch myself," Aiden said, but not to us. "From now on, I worry about my shit and you worry about yours." He shoved him again. "You said you were done with this!"

Sawyer bore it in silence.

Scoffing, Aiden turned his back on his friend and walked out.

"Sawyer," I began.

"Leave it, Val." He stomped over the remains of the shattered whiskey bottle and took another from the bar.

"Thank you," I said as he brushed past us, pulling him up short. "Thank you for jumping in and saving me."

"I wouldn't have let him hurt you." It was hard to hear him over the crackling fire. "You're a good person. Maybe the last good person in Nu Alpha and Zeta Rho. I don't know what Leighton was thinking when she let you in, but if you want my advice, get out. We were all different before we entered their perfect patch of Greek Row. Leave before they get to you too."

"Get to me?" I took a step toward him. "What does that mean?"

"If you don't know, you'll find out soon enough."

"But—"

"See you around, Valentina." He tromped out, bottle tipped to his mouth before he rounded the corner out of sight.

"Want to go after him?" Maverick asked.

"No." I took his hand once more. "Whatever we just walked in on is for Aiden and Sawyer to sort out. I meant it, Maverick. We're done."

Maverick bent and nibbled my bottom lip. A giggle made my mouth part and he swooped in, kissing the crap out of me. I was unsteady on my feet when we broke apart.

"We're done."

"YOU'RE DOING GREAT, ladies. One more mile."

The collective groans reminded me so much of my pledge time, I smothered a laugh.

It had been a month since that wild night and my dip in the pool. Since then, Aiden and I fell into our standard roles. Planning parties, activities, and the charity dinner. We didn't talk about anything else.

I maintained the same resolve with Eve, Sabrina, Kendra, and Teagan. Once or twice they brought up the club. A few "I'm not interesteds" finally shut down the conversation. Whatever they got up to was their business, and the business of finding out who Aiden Connelly truly was I left to Ryder's security team. They were smart, armed, and backed by resources. They could play detective. All I wanted to do was go to school, run my sorority, and curl up with my son, dog, and boyfriends at the end of the day.

"Smile," Jade crooned. The fit vessel of beauty, intelligence, stamina, and enigmas that we called Jade Ortega was literally running circles around us. She looped the running group, shouting encouragement at everyone.

"Jade, I love you," Ellie huffed. "But I also hate everything about you. Please don't take that personally."

Jade laughed without sounding the least bit winded. Honestly, it was obscene that she was barely breaking a sweat. "None taken. You should hear what my mom calls me on our weekend runs."

"Val," Chloe whined.

"No one escapes the physical requirements," I told her. "Not even me. All this running, training, and cooking with the sisters has me disgustingly healthy. I may even keep it up after I graduate."

"Would that be so bad?" Jade teased.

"Yes, because now I have to feel bad for all the cursing and swearing I did as a pledge."

They laughed at me.

"Is that your way of saying we're going to thank you?" Ellie asked.

Maeve jogged up to my side. "Why do we have to do this? Other sororities make you compete for how many shots you can down."

"We were formed in honor of Sally Hollenbeck. The powers that be decided we wouldn't be known for philanthropy or liver disease. We would emulate her by kicking ass in everything we do."

"If we don't kick ass, will we really not get in?"

"It seems harsh right now. Suffering through the test. Running, jumping, and working out. But all of this shows me how much you want it. Proves you won't give up and that you know what it means to be in it together. I did a lot of cursing as a pledge, but now I'm thankful Zeta Rho taught me how to stretch. It's how I reached new heights."

"Wow."

"Wow indeed," said Jade. "Well said. I agree completely."

In unison, my sisters said, "That's why they call you madame president."

I groaned.

MAVERICK

"The competition is this weekend and we don't have a bus. Can you drop the calm-and-collected act and freak out with me, please?" Cydney cried.

I cracked a grin. "It's not an act. I am calm and collected. The school will charter a new bus or I will. I'll pay for it myself if it comes to that."

"Oh." Cydney stepped into the elevator. "I forget how filthy stinkin' rich you are."

"You sound sickened."

"I am a bit." Though a smile played at her lips. "Guess that's one crisis averted. Now for the other fifty."

"Davis dropped out to focus on school and Bebop's crane stopped working. Both are situations we can handle."

"Need I remind you that the competition is this weekend?"

I blew out a breath. She was right. This was a disaster. We gave up our summers for this robot, and as the competition closed in, things started going wrong. We didn't have a club meeting that day, but Cydney and I were squeezing in an hour between classes to diagnose what was wrong with Bebop.

Cydney pulled ahead of me. "Maybe there's a problem in the code."

"There's nothing wrong with my code."

She stopped dead in the middle of the hall just to give me a deadpan look. "All right, Mr. Perfect. What could it be? We've put him through the course three times and he performed like a champ."

"'Cause he is a champ. We'll get him running again and Itzel will take over for Davis."

Cydney unlocked our door, swept in, and held it open for me. "Keep up the optimism. The calm-and-collected may rub off on me," she said as we made for our stations. "At least if we—"

Her scream jerked me to a stop but the sight of Sawyer would've done the same. The Sam lay spread-eagle on the floor. He looked peaceful, as if in sleep, and the reason for his slumber the needle sticking out of his arm.

"Cydney, call an ambulance!" I dropped down beside him. "Sawyer? Hey, man, wake up." I smacked his cheeks. Lightly. Then harder. "Wake up. You can do it, Sawyer. Don't go out like this."

His eyelids fluttered—the barest movement. A rasping groan rattled through chapped lips, and died just as quickly.

I couldn't rouse him again. Shouts, smacks, nor shakes. Sawyer lay still and pale, dying before my eyes.

"HOW ARE YOU HOLDING up?"

"I'm okay, Val. I'm not the one who overdosed in an empty classroom." I handed Cydney her coffee. The cup shook in her hands.

"Want me to come to the hospital?"

"No, I want you to go home and tell our son to never do drugs."

"I might wait until he knows what drugs are to get that promise out of him," she said, amused.

"By the time he knows, it's too late. While you're at it, tell him not to drink, gamble, and if he ever meets a guy named Aiden who wants him to join a club, knock the bastard out and keep walking."

"Yes, Daddy. I'll get right on that." Val sobered quickly. "Think this has something to do with the club?"

"Not sure. They haven't let me in to see him yet. I don't know if he'll talk to me, but I'll try. I got the feeling more than once over the last couple of months that Sawyer has lots of brothers, but very few friends."

"Well, *you* have me. If you need me to come, I will."

"I know." A white-coated man wearing a stethoscope came out of Sawyer's room. "I have to go. The doctor is here."

"Bye. I love you."

"Love you too."

"Hello." Doctor Walsh introduced himself. "You're the two who brought him in?"

"Yes," said Cydney. "Will Sawyer be okay?"

"He will. Mr. Burn is very lucky you two found him in time."

"Can I talk to him?" I asked.

"For a few minutes. He needs rest."

"I won't be long."

The doctor stepped aside for us. I side-hugged Cyd. "Want me to call someone to pick you up?"

"No. My friend is coming for me. I'll check on Sawyer and then leave you two to talk."

"All right."

Sawyer shifted as we came into the room. A pale imitation of him lay beneath the covers. Like a photocopy from a machine running out of ink. How didn't I see he wasn't well before?

Cydney bent over him. Whispered kind words in his ear and kissed his forehead. She patted my arm on the way out, leaving me to it.

"Hey." His voice was no louder than a thin, reedy whisper. "I remember you slapping me around. Thanks."

I pulled up a chair next to him. "I'd say anytime, but I'm hoping we never have to do this again."

He dropped his gaze. "I know what it looked like, Rick. Trust me when I say it was an accident. It can happen... after you get clean."

"Clean?"

"Your body can't handle the amount you were shooting up before. They told us that in rehab. Warned us." He laughed mirthlessly. "I should've listened."

"You went to rehab," I repeated as things began to click into place.

"For a year and a half."

I rubbed the bridge of my nose. "I see."

"Do you see? You understand why I refused to tell you where I was? Why I dropped off the face of the planet? My parents spent a lot of money to put me in a *discrete* facility. They didn't want this tarnishing my future. A stain I couldn't recover from." He sighed. "This will kill them."

"I understand that *this* wasn't any of my business. But we weren't trying to dig up dirt, Sawyer. We thought you were kidnapped."

"I... kind of was," he admitted. "Confessing that I had a problem didn't come easy. Even with the lengths I was going through to pretend everything was fine. I refused to take a look at what my act covered up. But Aiden saw it," he said. "Because of that file he keeps on us."

My head snapped up.

"Yeah, I knew about that. He was watching me so closely, he noticed my running times lagging. That I wasn't lifting as much or pushing as hard. I partied with the guys in the club, but my change in the house proved to him that the party didn't stop for me outside of Friday nights."

"So, he kidnapped you and made you go to rehab?"

"No," he replied. "Aiden contacted my parents who tried everything to reach me. I shut them out, insisted the booze and drugs were under control, and bitched at Aiden for ratting me out. The next thing I knew I was being thrown in the back of a van, and yes, that was my parents. They arranged it with Aiden believing the only way to get through to me was to haul me off for an intervention. It took a while, but eventually I agreed to go."

"Then, where was Teagan?"

"It's not my place to say." Sawyer sighed. "But I will say she left to take a break. College is intense and the Sallys and Sams turn that up to a thousand. It was a lie that she left to be with her mom, but it's not a lie that she was grieving."

I nodded slowly, putting the pieces together. "Aiden flipped out on you at the party because you relapsed."

"He warned me not to rejoin if I couldn't handle myself." He scoffed. "I couldn't."

"Hey," I said. "It's not easy. Especially being around that much temptation. You did your best and you'll keep doing your best today and each day after. That's all your family and friends want from you."

"Thanks," he gruffed, eyes shining. "For not judging me."

"I'm glad you'll be okay."

"I will be. Walsh says you saved my life. The least I can do is repay you, Rick, so go ahead and ask."

"Ask? Ask what?"

"The questions you're holding back because you're a good fucking guy. You don't have to. I— We owe you this and time is running out. Ask what you want to know about Aiden."

I rocked back in my chair. I wasn't ready for that offer and didn't have a response to go with it.

"Go on," Sawyer pushed. "Ask."

The name worked its way to my tongue. Unbidden, it forced itself out. "Leighton Lewis."

"Leighton? What about her?"

"Does Aiden know where she is or who is helping her?"

"Where she is?" He scrunched up his face and even that much pained him. "Leighton is dead. Didn't Valentina tell you?"

I studied him, searching down to his pores for a hint that he was lying. He stared back at me, eyes open and swirling with confusion.

"The files," I said instead. "Why?"

"That is actually easy to explain. The Sams are his guinea pigs."

"Excuse me?"

Sawyer tried to sit up and quickly thought better of it. I passed him a cup of water as he settled. "Aiden is working on a method. Program. Formula. I'm not sure what to call it, but it's meant to get an athlete to their peak performance. The mix of the perfect diet, training, vitamins, and downtime regimen that'll allow them to reliably play at their best at every game.

"As president of the Sams and considering all the requirements we have to complete, we're the perfect group to try his ideas and track his findings."

"He's experimenting on you?"

Sawyer didn't appear nearly as shocked as I was. "It sounds worse than it is. He doesn't make us do anything we don't have to do anyway. To be honest, his suggestions have helped a lot of the guys in the Sam house and on the football team," he explained. "They're his test group, and the club, those are his investors. Once he graduates, he'll have the money to launch his athletic company."

"It makes sense," I said reluctantly. "I'd hide a plan like that under a few encryptions too."

"Aiden is a tough guy to figure. He keeps everything close to the chest and won't give you a straight answer when messing with your head works just as well."

"Summed him up in one."

"But he's not a bad guy."

"He forced my girlfriend onto a ledge. Forgive me if I don't praise his genius."

"The fall wouldn't have killed her. Nasir, Hayes, Winston, and the others have jumped off the balcony into the pool dozens of times. No one was trying to hurt Valentina or y-you. That's not what the club is about." He broke off to indulge a coughing fit, cringing with the convulsions of his body. "It was started in 2005. The book doesn't name the founder but the president at the time was a graduate from Evergreen Academy. Wonder where they got the idea for a secret society built on money?"

"I can guess," I replied simply.

"My point is that Aiden didn't start this shit. He only took advantage of it. He seems like a complicated guy, but his motives are simple." Sawyer released a long, shuddering breath. "That's the truth, Rick. All of it. If it's not for you, tell Valentina and Ezra. They deserve to know what really happened to me.

"It's weird that you guys cared so much and you didn't even know me. Weird but..." His eyes brightened and he turned away from me. "Nice to know I have more friends than I thought."

"You do." I clapped his shoulder. "After you get well, we'll be on the other side. Supporting you."

"Thanks, man," he whispered. "Go on. Get out of here. You don't want to be stuck in this room with me."

"I can stay until your parents get here."

"No, I'm tired. I'm passing out the second you close the door."

We said our goodbyes. I left him to sleep and fished my phone out on the click of the lock.

"Val? Where are you? We need to talk."

I didn't want the truth like this, though I was right. Sawyer was the key learning the truth.

VALENTINA

"Guinea pigs?" Sofia joined me on the seat, using my lap as her footrest. "I admit my mind went to much darker, twisted places."

"He's refining the perfect athletic regimen and using the club to bankroll him. The other guys are likely his investors."

"Possibly," she murmured. "It doesn't explain the other people who've disappeared from the house. I doubt they all went to rehab."

"There always had to be another explanation because we knew Leighton and Aiden couldn't be behind it. Sallys and Sams have been dropping off the grid since they were children."

Sofia gave me a steady look. "Speaking of Leighton. Let's not pretend Aiden is cleared of all suspicion. Why would Leighton fake her death and then tell Aiden about it? Did he help her?"

"I don't know that we'll get to answer every question, Sof. What I do know is Leighton has no reason to hurt me and we've proven Aiden isn't messing people around either. Jacob and his team can worry about the rest."

"I like this." Sofia poked me with her toe. "You with your priorities in order and refusing to let anything knock you astray. You're taking command of your life, babe, and it's sexy."

I tipped off the seat laughing. "You are so nuts and I love it." I laid my head on her lap. "It does feel good to be free of this stuff. To know the truth—even just part of it—and be able to relax again."

"You deserve it, Val."

There'd always be the question of Leighton and Aiden's relationship and how he knew the details of that night. I'm choosing to let it go. They will not control me for another second.

"Val, you in there?"

"Yes," I called.

Blair came in and got comfy on Sofia's bed. "We need to talk pledges, La Presidenta. Technically, we don't choose until after the obstacle course, but we both have our favorites."

Sofia eased me off her lap. "I'll leave you guys to it. Pick a couple of winners."

Blair and I settled against the window. "Well?" she asked.

"If it's just about who I like," I began. "It's Maeve, Blakely, Ellie, Kara, Helena, Victoria, Grace, Lucy, Anna, Autumn, and Chloe. If it's the pledges who scored high on the test. Who topped the physical activities every week. The ones I like and who get along with all the girls, then it's Maeve, Blakely, Ellie, Victoria, Helena, and Autumn."

"I was going to say the same names, Val." She bumped my shoulder. "It has to be those six girls."

"Why?" I found myself asking. "We have room in the house for eleven. Anna lags behind on the runs now, but after a few months, she'll catch up. Chloe scored low on the test and are we surprised? That thing is evil. Why do we pretend these arbitrary challenges are what makes a sister?"

"They're not what makes a sister," she replied. "They're what makes a Sally."

MAVERICK

"Daddy, when are you coming home?"

"On my way right now." I plugged my other ear. My crew's celebration was getting rowdy. "Are you coming with Mommy to pick me up?"

"Yes. Pepper is coming too."

"Can't wait to see you guys. I've got presents."

Adam's cheers rivaled my team's singing. "We Are The Champions" had been on a constant loop during the three-hour drive. Couldn't blame them. Singing that song after a win made it twenty times more satisfying.

Fifty crises and we made it through them to deliver Bebop to the robotics competition. Monday Sawyer landed in the hospital. Tuesday the entire team went to visit him, finding him stronger and secure with his parents. Wednesday, Thursday, and Friday we replaced the shoddy parts that caused Bebop to break down, put him through the course again, and then set him loose on the competition where he placed highest in every challenge.

"Did you win, Daddy?"

"I did," I replied. "When we get home, we're going to celebrate. Are you ready? 'Cause we're staying up till ten o'clock and eating all the ice cream in the place."

Adam gasped.

"Eight forty-five," a dry voice broke in. "And two scoops of ice cream. Big boys need their sleep."

"Does this mean I'll be in bed by eight forty-five too?" I laced that with just the right amount of suggestion.

Val giggled. "If you're lucky. Will the bus be on time?"

I checked my watch. "We're about twenty minutes behind. I'll call when we're a half an hour away."

"Okay. Love you, babe. Adam and I are so proud of you."

"I love you both too."

I hung up and, finally, gave in. "Driver, crank it up."

"Yes, Ricky! About time." Cydney threw herself next to me, falling over my lap, and belted out the song in such a gratingly off-key pitch that I laughed until tears ran down my face. "Come on, Calm and Collected. Sing!"

I sang.

Fifty minutes later, our bus rolled onto campus. A line of cars and vans idled in the parking lot. I waved everyone off, thanking them for the hard work they put in.

"Is Valentina here yet?" Cydney asked. We were last to step off the bus.

"She'll be here soon."

"Want Rex and me to wait with you?"

"Nah. It's the weekend. Go home and bask in your glory." I lit on a familiar face waving for my attention. "Besides, there's a friend of mine. See you Monday."

"Bye."

I crossed the parking lot, rounding a gray van, and matched his smile with my own. I held up a hand to shake as one clamped over my eyes.

"Hey— *Argh!*"

Cloth covered my nose and mouth, seeping a sickly sweet scent into my body. Through the crack in their fingers, my friend's smile grew fuzzy, and then disappeared.

VALENTINA

"Daddy says we're staying up past my bedtime."

Oh, Daddy Maverick. What am I going to do with you?

"We are, baby," I said. "Forty-five minutes past your bedtime."

"Whoa."

Forty-five whole minutes was a lot to a little kid, and knowing my son, he'd make it twenty minutes in and then nod off on one of his daddies' shoulders.

And then I'll take Maverick upstairs and we'll have a real celebration.

I bit back my smile as I made the final turn for campus.

This was the start of the rest of our college life. Competitions, victories, cupcakes on the quad, hanging with my sisters, playing with my son, and loving my men.

I pulled into the near empty parking lot and called Maverick. The phone rang and rang until it went to voicemail.

"Hey, love. I'm here and the bus is here. Where are you?"

Ten minutes passed.

I called him again.

"You've reached Maverick. Leave a message."

Twenty minutes passed.

Adam asked for his father, peering at me with that sweet innocent face.

"He'll be here soon."

Thirty minutes passed.

I called Maverick's vice president, Cydney.

"Hey, Cydney. Do you know where Maverick is? I'm at the school waiting for him, but he's not here and he's not picking up the phone."

"He's not?" Alarm laced her tone which kicked my panic into gear. "We got off the bus together. He said you were coming soon and he'd hang out until you got there. Last I saw him, he went over to say hi to Sawyer."

"Sawyer?"

MAVERICK

"Sawyer, look. He's waking up."

My ear pressed to a hard, lined surface. A rhythmic *thump, thump, thump* sounded beneath me and a sudden jolt lifted me and smacked my head on the floor. The knock flooded clarity into my fogged mind. I was lying on a moving surface.

I went to grab my aching head and nothing happened. I tried again, straining in my bonds.

"Easy, Rick."

That voice. Hot, molten rage burned away the last of the haze. *I know that fucking voice.*

"It's just a bit of rope and chloroform." Hands grabbed and flipped me over. I gazed up into Sawyer's and Aiden's eyes. "Don't look so betrayed. This was the only way."

It was dark. Aiden and Sawyer were the sole figures I made out clearly. Another bump and the jolt kicked us up.

Van, a voice supplied. *I'm in the back of a van.*

"What the fuck... do you think you're doing?"

"It's simple really," said Sawyer. "Once we explain it all, you'll agree."

I glared at him. Less than a week ago, I sat next to his hospital bed while he fought tears and rivaled Casper the Friendly Ghost in complexion. Right then he looked ready to run a marathon. "You were sick..."

"As a dog," he agreed. "Did you know, you can measure the exact amount needed for someone to overdose without dying. All I had to do was fuck with Bebop, wait for you to show up to fix it, and then spill our story while you thought I was weak and vulnerable enough to tell the truth."

He lied? It was all a damn lie?

"Why?"

Aiden nodded, smiling that vile smile. I swore then and there I'd knock out every one of those teeth. "I told you it's simple. You see, it all started when I was alerted that someone hacked my encryption. Me," he repeated. "No one hacks me. It didn't take me long to trace the source back to you, and by then, I was intrigued.

"I knew what you were after. Ezra had Valentina suspicious of me and therefore you were too. I might've ignored you like I did the two of them, but anyone with your skills was someone I had to know."

"So, I joined your flag football team," Sawyer said, "and robotics. I did my best but you're not the easiest person to befriend."

"Didn't matter because I was working on something just for you," Aiden added. "You were looking for a mystery. Debauchery. The evil, cunning reason behind Sawyer's disappearance, so that's what we gave you. The club."

"Got lazy with that part. Didn't bother giving it a real name," Sawyer said.

"Cut me a break." They sounded like two guys kicking back for a chat. "I invented a secret society out of thin air, got the guys to help, fashioned you a fake drug and alcohol problem, and orchestrated it so on a dark, random night, Maverick Beaumont would walk up to another van all alone thinking he was safe."

"Why?!" I roared.

He shrugged. "I didn't have a choice. I had to fix a mistake. Playing football with you? We had to witness your fitness and stamina. Tossing poker chips and asking you *the question*. We found another way to give you the test." He tapped his skull. "To see how you reason. What you do when holding a bad hand. And club parties? Hello, bonding activities."

Aiden leaned over me, peering into my huge eyes. It was me. It was a trap from the moment Sawyer stepped into my elevator.

And I didn't see it.

"Somehow, we missed you." Aiden's intense gaze flayed me, stripping away my defenses and laying me bare. "Maverick Beaumont. It should've been you who walked through our door. Not Lennox. You," he whispered, "were meant to be one of us. A true Sam. And now, pledge, you will be."

My lips twisted. "Why in the fuck would I want to be one of you?"

He grinned back. "That's the best part. You'll find out exactly why in about ten hours. No more tricks. No more games. We're taking you to the same place Sawyer, Teagan, and so many Sallys and Sams have gone before. You'll find out why I have to do what I do, and when you come back, you'll help me continue what our very first president started all those years ago."

"Never. Going. To. Happen."

"Sawyer said the same thing," he sang.

"I did," Sawyer said. "Went down cursing, swearing, and promising on my mother's life. But I came around in the end. That's the thing, Rick. One way or another, we always give in." Sawyer reached behind him. "We've got a long drive."

He held up a cloth and a single brown bottle.

"You should get some sleep."

I thrashed, straining to get free. Buck them off. Anything.

"Why?! Why?!"

I yelled until I couldn't shout anymore.

<u>*Click here for the final book in the series, Redemption.*</u>[1]

---

1. *https://www.amazon.com/dp/B08LQTWMYD*

Keep In Touch

Join Ruby's Mailing list for news, teasers, and more: https://www.sub-scribepage.com/rubyvincentpage
Join Ruby's Facebook Reader Group:
https://bit.ly/3bNuCOq

ABOUT THE AUTHOR

Ruby Vincent is a published author with many novels under her belt but now she's taking a fun foray into contemporary romance. She loves saucy heroines, bold alpha males, and weaving a tale where both get their happy ever after.